All at Once

It's Complicated, Volume 2

Brill Harper

Published by Brill Harper, 2019.

This is a work of fiction. Similarities to real people, places, or events are entirely coincidental.

ALL AT ONCE

First edition. November 14, 2019.

Copyright © 2019 Brill Harper.

ISBN: 979-8223603474

Written by Brill Harper.

Sexy bad boys who do sexy bad things with their rough hands and the innocent virgins who love them. What's not to like? Sign up for Brill's News[1] so you never miss a new release. I won't spam you—I don't have time! You'll only get emails from me when there is a new release or a really great sale.

---

1. https://mailchi.mp/f440c4dede17/rockstarreaders

About

Her summer of raw emotion and unbridled passion...

Bliss Camden didn't know what she was signing up for when the employment agency sent her to the Wylder Colt Ranch as a live-in housekeeper for best friends and ranch owners, Levi Colt and Wylder Madison. The two rough, ready, and wild cowboys make her feel things she's never felt before...things she shouldn't feel about her employers. Wicked things.

Things they want to teach her all about.

It's wrong. It's primal. It's delicious.

She's not experienced enough to deal with one dominating cowboy, much less two. Besides, they'd never look twice at a frumpy wallflower like her...would they?

Author Confession: I see you, reader. I know what you want. Alphamallow heroes and awkward, nerdy heroines. It's a ranch, so there might be roping, riding, and wrangling. Ahem. And the swords. They touch.

Chapter One

Bliss

I don't know what my headstone is actually going to say, but I can tell you right now my cause of death is: *melted into a puddle of her own hormones due to exposure of extreme testosterone and sex pheromones.*

"Nice to meet you, ma'am," the tall, buff cowboy repeats, my hand still folded in his big, callused paw.

This would be the ideal time to respond with something that resembles manners or even basic coherency, but I have never been confronted with a man made up of such pure masculinity. Granted, I don't get out much. But, still.

He's just amazing. His name is Levi Colt, but he goes by Colt, I guess. He's six foot something, barrel-chested, and his jeans are painted on lovingly like a second skin of faded denim-blue. His smile is wide, genuine, and the little lines at his eyes tell me he smiles often.

"Ma'am?" he repeats.

"Sorry. It's nice to meet you too, Mr. Colt."

"Just Colt is fine." Right. He told me that already. Duh.

He lets go of my hand, and I'm bereft. I would like very much to just crawl up his body and burrow in. This has literally never happened to me before. I am usually unimpressed enough by men that I thought maybe I went the other way. But that didn't work either. (Her cherry Chapstick did *nothing* for me, but it was still a fun party.) So I assumed maybe I had no sex drive to speak of.

I was wrong. So very, very wrong. I have a sex drive that is currently running me the fuck over. This cowboy with surfer hair and eye crinkles has just ruined my panties.

"Let's get you shown to your room," he says, picking up my suitcase. "Follow me."

"Will Mrs. Colt be here soon?" I ask. The sooner I meet her, the better. I think. I hope I won't lust after her husband once I get my bearings. I'm not known for lusting. This is all so weird. But meeting the Mrs. should affect me like a glass of cold water. I hope.

"Nah, there is no Mrs. Colt, darlin'," he tells me. "Wylder, you'll meet him later, and I live in this big old house by ourselves. That's why we need a live-in housekeeper. We're not slobs, but this place needs a feminine touch for sure, and we're both single."

I assumed I'd be working for a family. Not two single men. It's a little nerve-racking. I guess if I feel uncomfortable after I meet the other rancher, I'll just leave. It's not like they hired me as a sex slave or anything.

I don't think.

I'm just being paranoid.

I hope.

And "big old house" is him trying to be humble. The house is brand-new and a veritable log cabin mansion. The timber logs are gorgeous, and huge floor-to-ceiling windows open up the view from every side. Mountains and prairie everywhere you look. I would think that the wide-open spaces would make me feel vulnerable since I usually prefer to tuck into nooks and corners whenever possible, but something about this place makes me feel safe.

"Colt" takes me upstairs to a bedroom bigger than my college apartment last semester. It's more than gorgeous. It's like a resort suite that I've only ever seen in pictures because the idea of me going to a resort is laughable. "Um, these are your maid's quarters?" I ask

"Well, technically, it's one of the two master bedrooms. But we figured you'd have more use for the en suite accommodations than either of us, so we put you in here instead. I took a smaller room down the hall."

"You gave me your room?" I squeak. Did he sleep in this bed? Did he *do* things to himself and other women in this room? How am I supposed to sleep imagining what may have happened in here? I'm having trouble remembering to breathe thinking about it, much less sleep.

"Trust me, there is no room in this house that isn't great. The smaller room actually has a better view, so don't worry about me. I still have my own bathroom, just not a sunken tub like the one in here."

"I just..." I look around. "I've never stayed anywhere so nice in my entire life." Nice seems like such a small, plain word. I feel like a cowgirl princess if that's a thing. If not, maybe Disney should get on it.

Colt smiles like I just told him he won the lottery. "We want you to be happy here. Nobody has time to go through another hiring process."

Not one person in my life has ever wanted me to be happy before. Certainly no one has put my comfort ahead of their own. "Well, your salary is more than generous, the list of duties doesn't seem too bad, though the house is bigger than I thought it would be, and the amount of time off I get is just short of ludicrous." I have so much time off that if I were not on summer break from school, I could still manage this job and my course work. Especially since the room and board is included.

"Yeah, we wanted a quality employee, so we're willing to pay. It's been a really rough couple of years." A shadow passes over his face, and I immediately want to do something to make him smile again. I'm such a dork. This hulking, handsome cowboy probably has women lined up to the highway eager to do things to make him smile. All he wants from me is three squares and fewer dust bunnies.

I get a quick tour of the upstairs, peeking in the rooms of both men. Colt wasn't lying—they aren't slobs. "Colt, this place looks really clean already. Why did you hire a live-in housekeeper? You could probably get someone in here once a week just to keep it up for you."

"We're busy outside all day. When we come in, we want a good meal, a clean house, and I don't know...a friendly voice and smile. We've been eating sandwiches and cleaning the house on our own, but we want to enjoy the evenings for a change. We've got a great entertainment setup in the den that we never use because we work too much and there's always more to do. You'll see the den downstairs. It's great. Surround sound. The works." He pauses. "You're absolutely welcome to join us in there at night to watch movies. Though, Wylder is a baseball fan so there will be a lot of that, too."

"Thanks," I answer, not sure why they want the maid to watch TV with them. I thought rich people preferred their help to operate in the background. This is the weirdest job ever, but I don't even care once I see the kitchen. The glorious, spacious, top-of-the-line everything kitchen. I could have a dance in it. What is that one cowboys do? "Boot Scootin' Boogie"? We could pack several rows of line dancers in this kitchen.

I can't help it, I geek out. "Oh my God!" This kitchen is better than some commercial kitchens. Those I've also only seen in pictures or on TV, but I have a Pinterest board of kitchen geekery. "All you guys have been eating is sandwiches?" I open the fridge. It's stocked with a lot more than fixings for roast beef on rye. The produce alone makes my heart race in anticipation. The arugula is prettier to me than any Monet painting in a museum.

"I went shopping before you got here so you'd have something to start with. You have a big food budget, though. Wylder and I like to eat, so whatever you still want to purchase is fine. I was hoping that by stocking it today, maybe you'd be able to make dinner starting tonight? It's been awhile since we've had home-cooked food. I know Wylder would appreciate it, too."

I almost hug him. "I would love to start tonight. Now. I'm so excited to try out that La Cornue range." I think it's the Chateau 120 model. Which makes me giddy. "I hope you guys filled out allergy forms in the binder the agency sent over with me, as well as food aversions."

"There aren't many of those. We're pretty easy to please. Maybe just not sandwiches for a week or two."

I waggle my finger at him, in my element at last. "You say that now, but you have not tasted my fresh baked bread."

His mouth practically waters. "You make bread?"

"I love baking. And cooking. If there are any special requests, just let me know." I pause. "Thank you for this opportunity. I'm going to make sure you two fall in love with my cooking, so I don't get fired if my cleaning isn't as great." I mean, I can do it. I'm just not Monica Geller about it.

He laughs, his blue eyes flashing. "I'm looking forward to handing you my heart in that case. I just won't bring out the white gloves."

He leaves, I watch him go, believe me, I watch him go, and then I get to work creating my first meal in the kitchen of my dreams. The ingredients are amazing, he must have gone to the farmer's market. Of course, being a small ranch, the beef is probably the best I've seen, and the freezer is full of it. The guys come in the back-door hours later as I'm setting their table. The binder notes said they prefer to eat in the kitchen.

I turn, ready to meet my other boss, hoping my apron isn't too dirty.

Well, fuck me.

He's just as potent to my girly bits as Colt. In a completely different way. His face is sharper, his brows dark slashes above his eyes, and he might even be a little bigger than Colt. His eyes, his eyes are darker than chocolate, and I feel like his gaze is a laser beam directed at me looking for secrets. His face is stern. So stern.

And that beard, though.

I swallow hard. There is a mad fluttering under my ribs. My breasts all of the sudden ache. This is insane. Twice in one day?

"So you're the new girl," he says in the kind of voice that rumbles inside me like too much reverberating bass in a rap song from a passing car.

Colt jostles him. "Nice, Wylder. She has a name." To me, Colt says. "Excuse him, he doesn't get out much."

Well, I know how that is.

"Hi," I manage. "I'm Bliss."

"Hmmm," he responds. Did his voice just thrum on my clit? What is going on in my body right now? Is any of what I'm experiencing a sign of impending stroke?

"Dinner is ready," I say cheerily, covering my sudden flush of unwanted nerves. "I'll serve and get out of your hair." I stir a pot that doesn't need stirring so as to look busy and not so addled. In fact, the pot is empty.

"Eat with us."

I pause the wooden spoon. It's not an invitation or even a request. It's an order issued by Wylder. A demand. And he walks past me to the sink, presumably to wash up. I put a cover on the pot in case he comes back my way and notices me stirring air.

Colt leans down near my ear, talking low and dangerously close, startling me and making me *very* glad I covered the empty pot. "Don't mind him. He doesn't have a lot of people skills lately, but he's a good guy. My best friend for as long as I can remember."

I nod, and he too goes to the sink. I can still feel his breath on my skin. I will not be surprised if my nipples have poked holes into my bra today.

I'm shaky, but I pull down another plate and serve the three of us up. We get seated, the guys across from each other and me in the middle. Colt compliments me on my cooking, several times. We discuss the Jeep in the garage for my use. We talk about the weekly schedule, my days off, my shopping budget...all while Mr. Taciturn says virtually nothing but, "Pass the potatoes."

It's a little uncomfortable and strange...Colt being so nice and Wylder being so aloof. Maybe he doesn't like me. Maybe he thinks I'm not good enough. Maybe dinner isn't to his liking, maybe—

"Does she know why she's really here?"

Wylder

THE SILENCE AROUND the table feels loud, but that's okay, the silence in my head always feels loud, too.

Colt is shooting daggers at me from his eyes, but the little miss doesn't look directly at me. She hasn't most of the evening. I've been looking at her though. Fuck me, but she's pretty. A round little body with the kind of tits that belong on a cartoon character, not a college girl. Not a college girl living with two full-grown men. No, tits like hers are an embarrassment of riches. If you believe more than a handful is a waste. I don't. I like my cups to runneth over. My new employee pretty much stepped out of my wet dreams and into my kitchen.

She can cook, too. I haven't had a meal like this since my ma's cooking.

But I'm pretty sure I'm going to fire Ms. Bliss Camden before the night is through.

There's no way I can resist the temptation. I make her nervous, which only ratchets up my desire for her. I like the way her pulse is racing in her throat. The way she fidgets when she feels me staring at her but is too docile to look up. She makes me want to challenge her and keep on challenging until I see her spark...just so I can dominate her right back to the submissive little thing in front of me.

Nobody has answered my question yet. It just lingers over the table like smoke. "Well, does she? Does she know why she's really here?" I ask Colt again.

Bliss still doesn't look at me, but she does look at Colt. Ain't that sweet? She thinks he's safe. "What is he talking about?"

A seldom seen frown crosses my best friend's face. "He's just messing with you," he answers, daring me to contradict him.

I lean back in my chair, pleasantly full from a fantastic dinner. "We came up with the idea to hire a live-in housekeeper because we wanted a wife."

She whips her head in my direction. Eyes wide. Mouth open. If she were on her knees, she'd be perfect.

"It was a joke," Colt says quickly. "We were joking. Wishing we had a wife. Being assholes about it, actually. Saying it would be nice if we had a little woman to take care of the house and our stomachs."

He leaves off a good portion of that conversation. Someone to take care of our dicks and blow us whenever we wanted was included. But he's right. We were being jerks. My mother, rest her soul, would have smacked us both upside the head for being so sexist about the cooking and cleaning being the duty of a "little woman." She would have tanned our hides for the blow job comments. Then she would have sent my dad in to finish us off.

I can't resist egging her on some more, though. "But then we decided we didn't want to deal with the other things that come with having a wife like...nagging, conversations about emotions, mothers-in-law. If we hired a wife, we could skip all the bullshit and just get the perks."

She flattens her lips into a firm line and glares at me. Oh, man, now my dick is twitching.

Colt blows out a heavy breath. "It was just a joke," Colt repeats.

I want to rile them both. I don't know why. "And then we decided we could just share a wife, since we share everything else. What do we need two for? Isn't that right, Colt?"

Look at that little pulse drumming in her neck. I want to put my mouth right there. I wonder if she'd let me bite her in bed. Leave my marks all over her.

"And then, when we stopped laughing, we decided we could just hire a housekeeper. Which is you," Colt answers. "And your job duties have been laid out in the agency binder, and we don't expect anything else from you that is not outlined in those pages. I'm sorry he's being a dick."

She relaxes. Colt has that way with women. People like him. He's naturally generous. I don't know why he's put up with my bullshit for so long. The one thing I can count on in this life is his loyalty. And he's got mine until his last breath.

But he's gonna be pissed if I ruin all the work he's put into getting our housekeeper. It took me a long time to relent on having someone else living here. Hell, we could make a lot more money if I relented about the permanent ranch hands, too. But I'm still having a hard time with that. It makes more financial sense to expand our herd and bring on full-time ranch hands, I know. But I'm wary of people living on my land anymore. I don't want to be responsible for anyone else.

Bliss wrings her little hands in her lap while she thinks about what she's gonna say. She's not comfortable with us yet. That makes sense. Finally she shrugs a little helplessly. "This is a little weird. I don't know how I feel about this."

"Honestly, the more we talked about it, the more we realized we just wanted a feminine presence in our house. That's all. It's not perverted or anything. Right, Wylder?"

She makes eye contact with me, a silent dare. I can't resist. "Nobody will touch you, little one. Not even if you beg."

Oh, but how I'd like to hear her beg. *Please fuck me, Wylder. Please let me suck your cock, Wylder. Please, let me come, Wylder.*

That last one gets me extra hard.

She turns back to Colt like she's aware that the direction of my thoughts has moved into unsafe territory for her. "So, you want me to keep house, cook, and what?"

Colt looks nervous. Damn. I shouldn't have pushed. He really wanted this to work. I probably scared her off when all he wanted was a little female companionship and the comforts of a real home—even if we had to pay for them.

We haven't had time to date since we started the ranch. And we don't have time now. A man likes to have a woman around, in his house. That's not sexist, I don't think. We just like women. Like their company. We only joked about the sex stuff briefly.

I answer for Colt. "Told you anyone we hired wouldn't understand."

She rounds on me. "Understand what? That you want a wife, but don't want to put any work in finding or keeping one?"

"It's not like that," Colt protests. "Someday, we do want a wife and kids. The whole thing. But right now, we're building this ranch so we have something to offer. We don't want anything from you that isn't in that binder."

"Not even if I beg," she says dryly.

I like her sass. Too much.

I like her long dark hair and the way she wears her clothes like she thinks she's hiding that lush figure. I like the way she's trying to hold her own with two older men even though she's scared. I like the way she cooks, and the way she leans her body toward my best friend but can't forget I'm in the room.

I'm going to burn in the fires of hell for my dreams tonight, because I can't decide if I'd rather watch her gobble down my cock or Colt's. It was just a joke that day we decided to hire us a maid. But now that I've seen our Bliss sitting between us, damn if I don't have a new fantasy.

"You're safe enough with us, kitten," I tell her.

But I'm lying. She's the opposite of safe. I should fire her right now before I lose control. Before I take what isn't mine. Before I make her give it all to me.

Chapter Two

Colt

When I enter the kitchen this morning and find Bliss cooking up a storm, the tightness in my chest since last night loosens. She's still here. I didn't trip over her suitcase and a certified letter from her lawyer. Breakfast smells amazing.

"You're still here," I say, coming all the way in the kitchen door and scraping my shoes on the mat.

She gives me a shy smile. "You've already been outside?"

"Milking, remember?"

"I thought you did that last night."

"Twice a day or the girls get ornery."

She blushes the sweetest pink. "I know absolutely nothing about ranching or farming. Sorry. I must sound like such a dork."

She's so fresh and pretty. I get the feeling nobody has ever told her that before, and unless I want to set off her pervert-meter again, I'm not going to tell her either. Wylder can be a real ass. There was no reason to freak the poor girl out. He just gets off on being dark sometimes.

Bastard.

"No shame in not knowing something."

She cracks a few eggs into a bowl. "I had no idea cows were so high maintenance. They sound like wives. I'm surprised you don't just hire them out, too."

I pour myself a cup of coffee and laugh. Then I hold up the cream pitcher. "Joke now, but I'm guessing your recipes that call for full cream will be enhanced by the freshness of having it delivered to you daily."

Her eyes get big. "Oh, man, I'm going to make butter. I can't wait."

We talk a bit about the process of getting our dairy. We sell some to the cheesemakers a few miles down the road, but we only have a couple girls at a time and use most of their daily offerings for ourselves. Bliss seems really interested in stuff that seems like it would bore a college girl, but she insists her first love is culinary arts. She's getting a degree in accounting for sensible reasons, but not because it's her calling.

When Wylder comes in, I watch his eyes darken looking at her from across the room. He's going to ruin this for us, I think. Part of me is still glad to see a reaction from him. He's been so closed off to life since the fire. The opposite of me in so many ways. After the fire, I got laid as much as I could. Drank as much as I could keep in me. Played as hard as I could without dying. Wylder went so far inward I didn't think I'd get him back.

Bliss plates our food and goes back to measuring ingredients. I guess she's getting a head start on another meal. I can't wait.

"Eat," Wylder demands, nodding at her chair.

"I'm not hungry." The way she says it, kind of bratty-like, sets off a spark in my best friend's eye. For the first time in a long time, he reminds me of the way he used to be.

"You always talk back to your boss that way?" he growls.

"Only when my boss is a sexual harassment lawsuit waiting to happen."

"Eat," he reminds her.

Damn if she doesn't plate herself up and join us at the table.

We eat in silence for a few minutes, me racking my mind to find something we can talk about that won't set off an argument from either of them. They're like oil and water.

"What does your boyfriend think of you working for two bachelor old men?"

I keep my tone playful. I'm drawn to her. I just want to know her more. Figure her out.

"Actually I don't have a boyfriend."

She says it so nonchalantly, but Wylder stops the fork a few inches from his face.

"The guys at your school must all be stupid," I say, willing him to keep to himself whatever he's thinking.

She shrugs. "I've never really had a boyfriend. My mom tells me I'm frigid." She hangs her head and covers her mouth like she can't believe she just said that. "I'm sorry. TMI."

"Why does she say that?" Wylder asks in his no-nonsense way. Not gentle, not coaxing, just out-with-it-he-doesn't-have-all-day.

Why would a mother say something like that to her daughter? I want to know, too. But I'd have shown some gentleness in the question.

"My mom has never *not* had a boyfriend. I'm a disappointment to her. She's the most popular woman in the trailer park, if you get what I mean."

With that, she pushes away from the table, and I stop Wylder from saying another word with one look. He relents and says something about changing into his other boots before we hit the fences. Which is bullshit, but at least he understands he isn't going to be much help right this very minute. Tact is required, and he doesn't have much.

When he leaves the room, I join Bliss at the sink, rinsing the dishes before she puts them in the dishwasher.

Her jaw is set and her movements very robotic. "You don't have to help me. I get paid well to keep this kitchen clean."

"I don't mind. You okay?"

She shrugs. "I'm embarrassed. I don't usually tell my life story to near strangers over breakfast. Especially ones that write my paycheck."

"Wylder had a pretty good upbringing, but me, I think I know where you're coming from. I was in and out of foster homes my whole childhood."

She glances up at me sideways. "Yeah?"

I nod.

She wipes down the counter next to the sink. "I used to *wish* for a foster family. My mom...she's no picnic, but her 'friends' were worse."

I want to fold her in my arms and hold her. I've got a real hero complex all of the sudden, I guess. I'd also like to find out more about these "friends" of her mother in case I need to commit murder on Bliss's behalf, but she's already closing down and it's best we leave this here for now. She'll open up when she's ready.

"Wylder is a lot different from you. I'm kind of surprised you guys are business partners."

Different doesn't even begin to explain us.

"He's been my best friend since I was eight. He's just rough around the edges."

"If you say so." She leans against the dishwasher. "He doesn't seem to like me."

"He likes you just fine. I promise."

She shakes her head. "He doesn't seem to like women in general."

"Now that is where you are wrong. Wylder loves women. He loves everything about women." She doesn't understand him. Not many people do. His fool heart is bigger than most, but he has to guard it more than some.

I take my finger and raise her chin up so Bliss looks at me and can see for herself that I mean what I say. "You're safe here."

She bites her lip shyly. "I know."

I'm becoming more and more fascinated with her with every moment that passes. Shit. This is not good. I'm telling her she's safe when I'm imagining how I'd ravish her if she were mine.

Wylder's ma once told me that when you meet the girl that's right for you, you're going to know it immediately. That's exactly how I felt when I first saw Bliss.

The best part is she has no idea how beautiful she is. She's self-conscious about her figure, but I'm a big man and like something to hold on to at night, and let me tell you, Bliss has a few things I wish I could hold on to.

I know without her saying so she's not ready for that. She's an untried filly, not yet broke to saddle. Some fillies need a gentle touch. An easy introduction to the saddle and the ride.

"I'll see you at dinner. We'll be too far to come in for lunch today."

As I make my way to the stable, I realize that part of the problem is that no one is better at breaking a horse than Wylder. And I wonder what that means for the three of us.

Bliss

AFTER OUR SECOND DINNER together, the men head out to do whatever it is men do after dinner on a ranch, and I clean the kitchen. My fantasy kitchen. I actually enjoy shining it up after making a mess of it. I rearranged some of the cabinets today, with permission, and I kind of wish I could just sleep in here at night, too. I love it so much.

It's a fine evening, and I wander out to the porch with a glass of lemonade when I'm through wiping spots that aren't there off my stainless steel fridge. I lean against the porch railing and gaze out at the ranch. Stars look brighter here than they do over the trailer park, that's for sure.

In the corral, a horse is furiously tossing its head and bucking, wildly doing everything it can to throw its rider. I'm curious about which of the men is willing to risk their neck to tame such a wild thing. I walk down the steps of the porch and make my way toward the corral, stopping at the corner of the barn so my appearance doesn't spook the horse.

My breath catches in my throat. Sitting on the jet black stallion is Wylder. His hair is as dark as the horse's. He isn't wearing a shirt, and even though the night air is cool, his tanned skin glistens with sweat. I guess horse training is physical work.

All I can focus on is lean, hard muscle, rippling and straining to handle the untamed beast. Wylder's legs tense under his faded jeans, cowboy boots digging into the sides of the horse, his face locked in grim determination. It's a wonder I can even stand because my legs feel like jelly. I stay to the edge of a barn and hold the wall for support. I can't tear my eyes off him.

He's so in control. There's a stillness to his focus. What would it be like to be on the receiving end of that kind of intense concentration? I squeeze my thighs together and try to remember that Wylder is not someone I should be fantasizing about.

When he turns the horse around, I quickly tuck myself behind the wall so he can't see me. Ridiculous, I know. I don't know why I'm hiding. He just makes me feel so vulnerable.

Reminding myself that he probably can't see me since I'm in the shadows, I slowly poke my head out again. His face is as hard as the rest of him, but damn, so incredibly handsome even at this distance.

The horse finally starts to settle down, and Wylder murmurs to the beast. His voice is low, deep, and syrup smooth. "That's a good boy."

As his strong hands expertly guide the reins and rub the horse's neck, I imagine what those hands would feel like running all over me. Guiding me. Telling me what a good girl I am. Watching him makes me feverish and like my skin feels too tight. The way his deep voice sounds so soothing, yet commanding, makes me wonder what he's like with a woman in his bed. Does he demand things, wicked things? Would a woman feel like she's being tamed? Eager and resistant. Scared and safe. Craving the reins, yet bucking the master.

He starts walking the horse toward the stables...shit, the stables. I'm standing right outside of them. Snapping out of my fantasy, I briskly walk back toward the house.

I bump into Colt on the way in.

"Hey now," he says, righting me

I shiver in his hands. My body has zero control. Zero. I would not be surprised if the blood in my veins has been replaced by the liquid currently ruining another pair of my panties.

"Are you okay, darlin'?" Colt asks, his big hands firming over my biceps. He hasn't pushed me away from him, even though my breasts are pushing into his chest.

I tremble and blame it on the night air.

Colt is probably more my speed, but he's way out of my league, too. I never even wanted to be in a league before.

I think I want to now.

I think maybe I'm made of want. My flesh and bones replaced with alien desire for things I don't understand.

"I'm fine, Colt."

"You certainly are."

I need to remember he's a flirt because that's how he's made. He probably treats all women to compliments and gentlemanly manners. I'm not special. It does no good to let myself pretend. I need to remember my place.

I back up and put some space between us. "I'm thinking about whipping up a quick cherry crumble. You interested?"

"I love cherries, darlin'."

For a minute, he sees right through me. There's no way he can know I'm a virgin, but somehow he does. The air between us is so thick, his innuendo floats like a low-hanging cloud. My toes curl as the ache inside me pulls low and deep.

I held onto my virginity by a thread growing up. It took an awful lot of artful dodging of men who had no business looking at me. My mom was drunk most of the time, and if her servicing didn't get the job done, there were those who thought I was some kind of alternate plan. Many of my nights were sleepless. Sometimes, I just ditched out my window and slept in an old tree fort I found in the woods. But sleeping in the woods isn't exactly restful if you're scared.

Looking at Colt, how handsome he is, how sweet and charming he is, I know he'd never take something that wasn't freely offered. Never try the doorknob belonging to a sleeping thirteen-year-old girl, cursing to find it locked. But I shrug my shoulders inward anyway, trying to make my breasts inconspicuous. Something I know will never happen.

A different woman might stand here and flirt with the cute cowboy who sees too much, but this woman doesn't know those kind of games. I nod at him, pretending not to know what he means, and get my ass back in the kitchen where I belong.

As I pull out the ingredients I need, I can feel my heart rate return to normal. I need to get my shit under control. This is a dream job for me. I need the money. I think I even need the open sky and the fresh air. I don't need to crush on two men who are never going to look at me like a woman.

I wouldn't even presume to know what kind of woman Wylder likes, but Colt probably likes sunny girls who smile a lot. Women who aren't afraid of their own bodies. Maybe someone who can give him a glimpse of the things he missed growing up in foster care. I certainly don't know how to give anyone that.

My breasts and my mother ruined any chance I had at a normal childhood. Developing early made me a target at school, and of course, a target at home for different reasons. But my mom killed any chance I had at normalcy when her behavior didn't stay in the trailer park.

She got caught giving a blow job to the father of the most popular girl in school, and I never recovered socially from that. That girl and her friends made sure of it. And she had a lot of friends. Or at least a lot of people who wanted to impress her. The bullying stopped just short of physical attacks, but the threat of it was ever-present.

Making friends who didn't mind being in my spotlight of shame was never going to happen for me. I was too dangerous to know. I had a couple acquaintances at work who were older and didn't care about high school drama, but none of them were close relationships, either.

I missed a lot, I think, growing up that way. I never learned what it was like to be a normal girl, so I know even less how to be a normal woman.

For the first time, I'd like to learn.

Both men enter the kitchen as I'm dishing up the dessert.

"Smells good," Wylder says. "What are we having?"

I don't answer. I physically can't. All my mind is capable of doing is replaying the scene of him on the bucking horse, clad only in boots, jeans, and a cowboy hat. An image that will be branded onto my brain forever. Heat spreads throughout my body.

"Cherry crumble, I think," Colt says, saving me from having to form words around a tongue tied in knots.

Wylder smiles, but it doesn't reach his cold, dark eyes. "I love cherries."

It doesn't sound so flirty when Wylder says it. Despite the danger his mere presence implies, I melt more from the inside out. My underwear can attest to this.

I fake yawn. "I didn't realize how tired I am. I think I'm going upstairs now. Enjoy the dessert."

I don't wait for the command to "sit" or "eat" that will come if I gave him the chance. Instead, I bolt, using the artful dodging skills I acquired in my youth.

I don't lock my door. It's not them I'm afraid of. It's me.

And no matter how fast I run, I'll never outrun myself.

Chapter Three

Wylder

"I'm not gonna lie, Wylder, it's pretty bad," Colt tells me, kneeling on the ground, his sleeves rolled up, concern etching lines into his usually relaxed face.

The young foal he's tending to is scared and hurt, her outstretched leg wrapped in bandages. He's right, it's pretty bad. "Have you considered that maybe the best thing is just to..."

"Yes," Colt's voice is hard and curt. "I've considered it. We'll wait a while to see how it goes, though."

I nod, but I'm not sure time is going to help.

"It's not broken, Wylder," Colt accuses, the words are stretched thin over his vocal cords, but the emotion pokes right through.

"I know. I just don't want you to get your hopes up." A good rancher has to have empathy for his animals, but sometimes the best thing for them is a humane and quick death. It's never easy to make those choices, but it's harder on Colt.

"She'll be all right," he says.

Fuck, I hate when shit bothers him. He doesn't talk much about his early childhood, the years before I met him, but it doesn't take a genius to realize why he hates to see anyone or anything helpless or hurting.

I keep my own voice calm. "Her leg is in pretty bad shape. She might be suffering, Colt."

"I just can't do it tonight," he grinds out. "I have to give her a shot."

He looks up at me and we share an understanding that many people never experience. I'd walk across hot coals to erase the sadness in his eyes. Colt is the only family I have left in this world. I don't think I'd be alive today if he weren't here.

"Dinner was good tonight." I aim for changing the subject.

He gets up and brushes the hay off his jeans. "Dinner is good every night. She's a fantastic cook."

"She's not that great at cleaning."

He shoots me a look. "Like you fucking care about her cleaning. I saw you going back for thirds on that casserole. She's a great find. We're lucky we found her. And that she's stayed this long."

"What you mean is we're lucky I haven't scared her off." Yet. It's been a couple weeks almost.

"Sometimes I think you're trying to."

"I don't want her to go." Not exactly. "I just..." I glance at the wounded foal. "Don't go getting attached to her. She's not for the likes of us." And I don't want him getting hurt.

"I know she's only here for the summer. I can't make promises that I won't get attached to her cooking, but my heart isn't in danger. Just my stomach."

"Sure thing, Hoss." We check the other stalls like we do every night. The steers make us the money around here, but it's the horses that make this life what it is.

He flips the light off. "Maybe it's you that likes her too much."

I wince as we head out. "We can barely stand to be in the same room." It's a balmy night. Maybe it will rain.

"Don't be stupid. I know you better than that. You push her away like you're some gruff asshole so you don't have to get close."

"I am a gruff asshole."

"Well, I'm not going to argue that. But you push her. Why is that, I wonder?"

We start walking toward the house. I like this part of the evening when chores are done, we've been fed, and I can take pride in the spread we've been tasked to be caretakers of. I almost lost it all. Lost my family, the old ranch, and was losing my damn mind, but Colt dragged me out of the hole and made me live again. This land is more than dirt and a good view—it's everything. To both of us.

I take off my hat and run a hand through my hair. "I'd think you'd be glad I push her away. Less competition for you."

He snorts at that. "Competition. I'm pretty sure if we ask her right now who she'd rather spend time in the hay with, it wouldn't be you."

"Exactly. You proved my point."

"Oh, so you're being an asshole for my benefit. Thanks so much."

I laugh and punch him in the arm. "She ain't stayin'. Don't get attached."

"I know." Just like he knows that foal probably won't make it. But it doesn't stop him from hoping. Nothing stops him from hoping. I don't know how he holds on to it the way he does.

And he's hoping for Bliss.

The trouble is, if she were staying, there would be competition. We've never fought over anything. What if she drove a wedge between us? Now, when everything is finally working out our way. We're building something good here. Something we put our literal blood, sweat, and tears into. I'm not risking that over a woman.

Not even if she's perfect.

Which she's not. She's got more baggage than the claim carousel at the airport. She's leery of men and afraid of her own body. And she turned my damn socks pink in the washing machine. She's not perfect at all.

We slow as we get closer to the house. We both know we're not done talking about the little miss and can't finish our conversation inside.

Colt starts and stops himself from saying something.

"What?" I ask. "Just say it."

"I don't think she wants to go back. She doesn't even like college. She only goes because she thinks a degree in accounting will give her security."

"I suppose she told you that."

"Actually, yeah. She did. She hates her accounting classes, but she says she's good at math so she figured it would be smart. She likes cooking. Said she used to dream about being a chef, but didn't think it was practical."

"Why are you telling me this?"

We both know why. He thinks if I hear she's looking for security, I'll want to take care of her. His weakness is rescuing everyone, mine is taking responsibility for everyone around me. I only know this because he made me take a personality test online with him.

But damned if that test wasn't true.

What I don't understand is why he wants me to want her.

"She might stay, Wylder. She could stay."

I stop walking, watch the shadows grow longer as the moon starts her rise. As a rule, Colt and I don't talk about feelings. We don't really need to, anyway, since we know each other well enough to sense what the other is going through. But I don't understand him right now, which is unusual. I've never gone willingly into a feelings talk, but I don't think I have a choice. "You want her to stay?"

"So do you."

"You want her to stay for me or for yourself?"

Colt's no more excited about talking about feelings than I am. He shuffles his boot over a rock. "We could let her choose."

"Right. And say she chooses me. You just gonna be okay with that? You're not going to break down my damned door when you hear me fucking the girl you want for yourself?"

His jaw tightens the way I knew it would, but he shakes his head, refusing to be drawn into a fight, though I know right now, he's picturing me in bed with her. "We could let her choose not to choose."

I ain't often surprised, but my eyes blink too rapidly. "Are you fucking serious right now?"

We joked about it the one time, sharing a wife. But we're both too damn possessive to be brother-husbands or whatever you call it.

"Just think about it, okay?"

"Think about what? Quit pussy-footing around and tell me what's going on in that mess you call brains."

"I'm thinking that for the first time in years, I've seen you show real interest in a woman. Because however well you think you are hiding it, I know you better than you know yourself, and you want her."

I want to deny it. We're too old for her. She's too innocent for us. Especially for me.

But he doesn't wait for me to interrupt him and keeps on talking. "And I want her, too. And if I thought you just wanted her for a quick fuck because she's got a nice rack, I'd be pissed as hell. But since I see right through your shit, I know what you really want is to court her."

"Court her? Did you hit your head today?" He's talking like my ma used to.

"So I say, we *both* court her." He is fucking serious right now. I'll be damned.

"Maybe Bliss put something in your sweet tea. Some kind of mind-addling poison."

"We could show her what it would be like for her if she stayed."

Colt

"WHAT IT WOULD BE LIKE? It would be like her being stuck in the middle of nowhere with two perverts who are too old for her," Wylder says on a growl.

Oh, he's ornery now. That's okay. This is how it works with him. He gets pissy, I say things he pretends not to agree with, and then later, he comes around.

All I have to do is stay logical now. "She doesn't like the guys her age. She doesn't even date them."

Wylder pinches the bridge of his nose. "I don't think it's the guys that are stopping her from dating. She's scared of men."

Well, no shit. "You think I don't know that? But she's already feeling comfortable around us, despite how much you try to be an asshole to her. She laughs and smiles all the damn time now, and she stopped wearing as many clothes as she could get on herself and still move."

When she first got here, it was layers and layers of armor. The last few days, she's down to a t-shirt and jeans most days. The shirt is still way too big for her, but she doesn't act like she might have to be on the run with just the clothes on her back anymore.

Wylder's jaw is working. Tense and square. But hell, when isn't he tense and square? Lately, that's all he is. "I've only ever seen her laugh or smile when she's in the kitchen," he finally says.

"Stop trying to intimidate her all the time and maybe you'll catch one in a different room. They sure are pretty."

He meets my eyes. "This is fucked up. You really don't think you'd get jealous? What is she supposed to do, trade off bedrooms between us? Do we make a calendar? This will never work. How are we going to handle holidays? I fuck her on Christmas and you get Thanksgiving?"

"Actually, in my head, I thought we'd switch off what nights we go to *her* room. But that's putting the cart before the horse. We're courting her, not bedding her."

"We're not courting her."

He makes to stalk back into the house, but I grab his shirt and pull him back. "It won't work if we don't try." He shrugs my hands off him, but I keep talking. "I don't know a lot of things, but I do know that I care about that girl, I know you care about that girl, and I know I would die before I let someone come between you and me. But sometimes, when I think about her going back to school in September, it sure feels like a piece of me is already dying. Just...think about it. Please."

"Not ten minutes ago, you told me your heart wasn't involved."

I should have something to say to that, but he's right. Hell, he's always right about me. Which is annoying as hell. I brush past him and head in alone, beating him into the house.

That was the hardest conversation I've ever had. One that could have gone to shit fast. Maybe it did. Maybe things won't be right in the morning, and I just trashed my partnership. I'm glad I don't pass Bliss on my way upstairs to my room. I need to be alone. To think.

Or maybe not think. Thinking is what got me into this mess.

She's barely been here two weeks, and I've risked everything for the chance to court her. And, yeah, that's old fashioned and dated. But it sounds right for Bliss.

Hell, she might not even want either of us. But I don't think that's true. I think she's confused about how she feels and has had some bad shit in her past, but I know she's attracted to me. And the way she gets all fluttery and pink around Wylder, I'd say she's attracted to him, too.

I think about her pretty eyes when she looks up at me and smiles or laughs at something I said. It's like the sun punching a hole in the clouds when she laughs. I find myself thinking of things to make her smile all day long like some dopey junior high kid with a crush.

I turn on the shower as hot as I can stand it and let the water wash away all the stress from the foal in the stable, from my talk with Wylder, from all the shit that doesn't get done that needs to, and instead think about what it would be like if Bliss really were mine. Ours.

My dick plumps up at just the thought, and I haven't even focused on the fantasy part yet.

I soap my body up, saving my dick for last. She thinks of me like some damned knight in shining armor, and God knows I want to fix all her problems and save her. But I'm no saint. I've got urges. What would she say if she knew about those? She's so shy about men. About her body.

I groan. What would she think if she knew her knight in shining armor likes to imagine pounding her tender pussy with jackhammer thrusts until she forgets her name? Until her whole damn existence is focused on me.

I soap up my cock, hardening as my hand moves on the shaft, thoughts of my pretty housekeeper in my head. The images in my head are vivid. Rated X. Imagining her hand on me instead of my own, my hand moves faster, thrusting into my soapy fist. My hips start thrusting and my forehead beads with sweat. My body is primed and ready to fuck.

I've never gone this long without sex before. I even went out last weekend with the intention of a good dick wetting. But as much as my body wants release, it wants Bliss more. I couldn't even get hard at the bar when Lacey June came in wearing a short skirt and no more wedding ring. Bliss has got me all tangled up inside two weeks. It ain't right.

It's not her hand now in my fantasy, it's her tight sheath squeezing me while she moans my name. I spread my legs wider and jack furiously, breathing an effort now. I feel the cum building up deep inside me, and I suppress the urge by squeezing the tip of my cock. *Not yet. Gotta make it last.*

I imagine the heat of her tight pussy, dripping wet and spread open while taking me in. I groan. Words from a bad porno tumble out of my mouth. "Yeah, baby, fuck your boss's cock...this cowboy needs your pussy so bad."

My cock is rock hard now and a dark, angry red from my abuse. I need to come, the muscles tensing in my quads and back. But still, I don't want to let go yet. I imagine her legs wrapped around me, her heels digging into my waist. I see flashes of her pretty smile mixed in with darker, earthier ones, flashes of ripe tits and a round ass. The fire she gets in her eyes when she's holding her own against my best friend. The idea of waiting my turn when she's in his room, when he's inside her and I can hear them.

I grunt, trying to hold back my orgasm. "You feel so good...take it, Bliss...take it all." My hand is slamming in punishing strokes now, and the tingle in my balls becomes unbearable.

I imagine her coming around me. Squeezing me. Screaming my name. The tingle spreads to my cock before it explodes in a thousand shards of pleasure. My whole body floods with pure white heat. "I'm coming, Bliss...coming deep in your little pussy." My hips jerk as I come hard, squirting long, ropy strands on the tiled wall.

Chapter Four

Bliss

Do you know how much laundry cowboys go through? I lug the basket, heavy with denim, up the stairs, stopping first by Wylder's room to drop off his folded clothes, then into Colt's room.

As I enter his bedroom, I notice his bathroom door is open halfway, but it isn't until I'm opening his dresser that I realize the shower is running. Whoops. I thought they were still outside. Backing up to leave, I'm brought to a dead stop when I hear him speak. Shit, he knows I'm here.

"Yeah, baby, fuck your boss's cock...this cowboy needs your pussy so bad."

Is he...with someone?

My face goes molten hot, and I want to run out, but something perverse keeps me rooted to the floor. I look above his dresser at the mirror reflecting his image from the bathroom. He's *alone* in the glass-encased shower, whipping his hand up and down his cock...his huge cock. Not that I'm close enough to see it in great detail, but I guess that kind of speaks to how big it is.

I'm the biggest jerk in the world for invading his privacy, but I still can't move.

He's beautiful in the way men are. Corded muscles bulge in all the right places. Tree trunks for legs holding up the round butt that fills his jeans so well. He's masculine perfection.

I'm mesmerized by the sight of his big hand stroking relentlessly on his cock. He's not gentle with himself at all. There's so much power in his body, all of it focused on an impending orgasm. I'm really intruding, but I don't think anything in the world could pull me away now. I'm just as focused on his impending orgasm as he is, my core clenching on the emptiness between my legs.

"You feel so good...take it, Bliss...take it all!"

My name. He just said my name. He's fantasizing about *me* in there. A hot tingle swells inside me, starting at my clit and working its way through my center. At the same time, chills shoot through the rest of me, making me shiver and break out into goose bumps. I start backing up slowly, quietly.

I have to go. Run. Get out of here. Tamping the urge, I take careful backward steps.

Until I bump into a hard body behind me and am wrapped in tight bands of muscular arms.

Wylder

"SHH," I TELL THE LITTLE miss as she squeaks, my arms tightening protectively around her. "You're going to give yourself away."

"Oh my God," she whispers. "I didn't know he was in here. I thought you were both still in the barn. I was just dropping off laundry. Please, let me go. I should leave."

"I don't think so, sweetness. I thought about passing by and letting things unfold however they might, but turns out I couldn't. I wanted to be a part of whatever naughty thing you were up to in here."

She gasps. "I didn't mean to."

Oh, she feels good trembling in my arms. "Maybe not, but you might as well stay for the climactic finish."

I expect another argument, but we hear a loud groan from the bathroom, and she slumps against my chest. Her chest heaving and her nipples poking through her shirt. In the shower, Colt has one hand on the tiles, his head bent, and he's furiously stroking. Atta boy. Go get it, Colt.

I whisper low into her ear, "Do you like to watch, Bliss? He's with you in his head. How does that make you feel?"

She shudders on a breath. "I should go." But she doesn't struggle out of my hold, just presses harder into my chest.

She's the perfect mix of innocent and dirty. She's got them both bottled up together inside, shaking her up like bubbles in a champagne bottle. I want to be there when she pops that cork. Hell, I want to be more than there. I want to mop up her spills with my tongue.

One more groan from Colt. "I'm coming, Bliss...coming deep in your little pussy."

We both hold our breath watching his body tense and release. You can't make out much detail, but my mind fills in the rest. I've seen Colt's naked body plenty of times at the swimming hole. I've never seen him turned on, never watched him come. My own dick is getting button imprints from my 501s, and I'm sure the housekeeper knows exactly what is pressing into her. The air is charged with sex and desire. Hers. Mine. Colt's.

He's struggling for air right now, and his massive body twitches as aftershocks of a really good come overtake him. It feels wrong, holding the woman he wants while we watch him in a private moment. It also feels right in all the wrong ways. I've never been a voyeur before, but it stokes a hunger I didn't know existed. I want to watch him do more. To himself. To Bliss. I want to watch her shatter when she can't take the teasing any longer.

The sound of water turning off causes her to stiffen, and I let her go so she can run out of the room.

I still don't want to court her, but I sure the hell wouldn't mind this summer taking a different turn. We can send her back to college with a whole lot more experience if she's game.

I don't run out. Instead, when Colt exits the bathroom with a towel slung low on his hips, he finds me standing in the same spot with my arms crossed over my chest.

"Jesus, Wylder. What the hell?" he says, startled.

"Been thinking about what you said."

He cocks his head. "Yeah? And."

"Let's take her to town tomorrow night."

"Why? I thought you didn't want to court her."

"I don't."

"Seems like a date to me."

"The Hound Dog isn't really a dating kind of place."

"It's the only thing we've got in town. So you want to take her out, but it's not a date."

"Yep. I guess I do."

"You're a strange fucker, but fine. Tomorrow, the three of us go to the Hound." He crosses to his dresser and pulls out a pair of track pants, then looks at me. "Are you wanting to braid my hair? Why are you still here?"

When I realize the reason, I flip him off and go.

I wanted to see him drop his towel.

◆

Bliss

I'M NOT SURE WHY I agreed to come to the saloon with Colt and Wylder. Pretty much anything Wylder suggested I went along with today, desperately afraid he was going to tell Colt that he caught me spying on him.

I should tell Colt myself, which I guess is another reason I agreed to come with them to the Hound Dog. It seemed like something that would be easier to do after a few beers. I need to do it before Wylder outs me. It's not good to let him have blackmail material, though I spent a lot of time last night thinking about what he might want me to do to keep my secret. What kind of perverse acts I'd be willing to do for his silence.

And of course, when I tear my mind off indecent ideas about Wylder, it goes right back to Colt fantasizing about me while he stroked himself. The shape of his body. The strength and force of his passion.

It's been a super long day.

The Hound is a dive, just like they told me it would be. I expected country music, but instead a jukebox is blaring out Metallica. The floor is sticky, the tables dirty, and the whole place reeks of stale beer, sweat, and cigarettes. I pause while my eyes adjust to the dim light. A layer of smoke hovers in the air. Apparently, no one much cares about the smoking ban at the Hound.

A big man sits at the bar, tattoos flowing up his big muscular arms. I'm immediately tense. Maybe this was a bad idea. I spin around and am greeted with Colt's broad chest all of three inches away from my nose. Startled, I take a couple steps back and crane my neck up to look at him. He's looking down at me with an amused, devilish smile across his face. "You okay?"

I nod. Sure I am. My face heats as I remember him calling my name in his shower last night.

"You don't have to worry about that guy," he tells me as if he knows the thoughts that ran through my head when I saw the burly man at the bar. "We wouldn't have brought you here if it wasn't safe."

"He just looks like someone I knew once."

"You trust us, right?" Colt looks rugged, especially with the five o'clock shadow he's sporting. He's got on a t-shirt and jeans, which fit him like skin, and his hair is tousled in a sexy, natural way that suggests just rolling out of bed.

But, yeah, I trust him. And Wylder. Mostly. Wylder would never hurt me, I know. But I don't think for a minute he won't be happy to use emotional blackmail on me. He suddenly turns to catch me staring. I blush and smile nervously, but he doesn't drop his gaze. A strange anticipation in my belly leads to a trembling vibration even lower. My stomach churns anxiously.

"Let's get a table."

Colt and I sit while Wylder goes up to the bar to order a pitcher. "Why are you so jumpy tonight?" he asks me.

"This place reminds me of where my mom worked for a while."

"And that wasn't a good place."

I shake my head. "She took me to work with her sometimes. She said she got better tips when I was there."

"When you were little."

The shame singes across my chest like a burn. "I was sixteen. She made me wear...I don't even know why I'm telling you this. She made me wear tank tops that were too small."

"Did she make you do anything else?" His voice is laced with concern. And anger. Finally, someone besides me is angry at my mom.

"No. I just sat at the bar and did my homework. But I knew they were looking at me."

"Jesus, Mary, and Joseph. I'm sorry. Do you want to go home?"

Home. Wow. Two weeks and I already am gripped with an instant longing for the ranch. Which is a pit stop in my life, really. Just a summer fling with stability. "I'm fine."

"We can leave right now, Bliss."

A pitcher and three glasses appear in the center of the table. "We're leaving already?" Wylder asks, taking a seat on the other side of me.

"No. I'm fine."

"What's wrong?"

"She's uncomfortable here." Colt takes my hand under the table and squeezes it gently before letting it go.

Wylder sizes me up. "Why are you uncomfortable here?"

"It's nothing," I answer. "I'm fine."

"The Hound reminds her of a bad time," Colt persists.

"Her mouth isn't broken. Let her talk." He pours our beer calmly and waits for me to answer as if he doesn't question that I will.

I wish I were confident like he is. He's sparked something inside me, though. "This place reminds me of the assholes who used to tip my mom extra money to look at my underage breasts in a tank top, okay? Are you satisfied now?"

He slides my glass over to me. "So, you going to let them win or are you ready to fight back?"

"Wylder..." Colt kicks him under the table. "Have a little sensitivity, will ya?"

"She doesn't need sensitivity. She needs—"

"What makes you think you know what I need, Wylder?" A hint of fear rises in my chest at being so openly defiant to him, and I don't understand it.

His face is unreadable. "Everyone's got demons. You don't get to choose which ones are assigned to you. The only thing you get to choose is if you fight 'em or let them have your soul. You seem to me to be more of the fighting kind."

"This conversation feels a whole lot deeper than the 'let's go have a beer at the saloon' that was suggested to me."

My attempt to lighten the mood does nothing to the dark, penetrating gaze of Wylder. He's looking right into me. What does he see?

"How do you fight your demons?" I ask him.

He takes a long drink. "I don't. I like my demons just fine."

Colt looks at his friend with a different kind of intensity. Then he turns those warm eyes on me. "We can leave. It's fine."

I shake my head. It's like "Eye of the Tiger" starts playing inside my head. "No. He's right. I don't want to be scared when there's nothing to be scared of. The past is the past."

"I promise you that you never have to be scared with us. We'll protect you. Always."

"Who's gonna protect her from us?" Wylder ponders, pouring more beer into my glass.

"Damn it—" Colt says.

But I pat his hand. "It's okay. I see right through him now."

Wylder cocks his head. "What do you think you see?"

"You think you're toughening me up."

"And why would I want to do that? I think I like you soft and scared."

His direct gaze is in opposition with his silent threats. I think he's daring me. Does he think I will cower? Do anything to cover up my secret? What is it that he would suggest I do to keep Colt from finding out about last night?

The ideas are intriguing and also scary as fuck. Mostly because I would probably do whatever he wanted. Which means I need to fix this myself.

I gulp down my beer and slam the glass on the table dramatically. "Colt, I'm sorry, but last night I watched you masturbating in your shower. Also, I heard you say my name when you did it."

Chapter Five

Colt

It's like a bomb dropped in the middle of the table. "You what now?" It's not like I'm clutching my pearls or anything, but I don't have any idea where this is going. Should I be mad? Did she like it? Was she flattered? Pissed off? She's here, with us, so it must not have scared her away.

Wylder smiles bigger than I've seen in a long time. "Kitten, you sure know how to surprise a man."

I have a feeling he's talking about himself more than me. What the hell is going on?

She shoots him a look and then turns her doe eyes back to me. "I'm really sorry." So Wylder knows already. Interesting. Her lower lip trembles, and I forget for a minute I'm shocked and just want to scoop her up and pull her onto my lap. "I was putting your clean clothes away and didn't realize you had come back in from milking. I should have run out, but—"

"But you were soapy and naked and calling her name," Wylder supplies helpfully.

I swing my head his direction. "Why were you there?"

"I came in before the big finale. I was in the hall when I noticed her creeping on you. I figured I'd be able to tease the little miss about being a voyeur for weeks, but she just took all my fun away." He leans his chair back on two legs. "Now I'll have to make do with watching you squirm when you try to talk your way out of the reason her name was on your lips when your hand was on your cock."

She's trying so hard to be brave and be adult about this, so even though I'm embarrassed, too, I settle for the truth. "I took matters into my own hands because I'm a guy, and we do that kind of shit when there's a pretty girl around." Or if the day ends in Y.

"You think I'm pretty?" she says it soft-like, stirring up those damn knight in shining armor impulses inside me.

"It's not a matter of opinion, darlin'. Fact is you're a beautiful young woman. And I appreciate your honesty. I know that must have been tough to admit you were there."

"It felt disloyal to keep it from you."

I hear Wylder's chair come back to rest, but I don't pull my gaze away from her. Loyalty is really important to Wylder, and I bet she just gave him something to think about.

"Do you hate me? For intruding?"

"What I would hate is if it made you think less of me or made you embarrassed to be around me. Since you're here tonight, I'm guessing we're good?"

She nods. Then she looks at Wylder, and her face sharpens under his gaze. "What?" she asks him.

"You've got guts, I'll give you that."

She shrugs. "I can be scrappy when I need to. That's how I survived this long."

She's a survivor. She's had to be, and that pisses me off. What's worse is that it kills me to know she doesn't need me. I want her to need me even though I should be glad she can handle things on her own.

We order another pitcher, but Wylder stops drinking. He's driving tonight. It doesn't take but a couple more glasses for Bliss to loosen up even more. She's not drunk. Not really. But she's relaxed, even poking fun at Wylder now and then.

She's laughing at a story from our misspent youth when he tells her, "Take your hair down."

Her smile stays plastered on, but it's confused now. She looks at me to make sure I heard him say it too. "What?"

"Take your hair down," he repeats in a low voice. His eyes are glittering like dark glass.

"Why?"

"I like it down. I want to see it."

Her lips press into a firm line but she's captivated by the way he's looking at her. The tone of his voice. He's just commanding all her attention. "Why do you think you can order me around?"

"I've been accused of being bossy a time or two."

"Only a time or two?"

Oh, hell.

But the way he is smiling at her. I haven't seen him so relaxed in a long time either. So I let this play out without getting in the middle of it. For now.

She's holding her own, but she's definitely rattled. It doesn't take a genius to see he's got an effect on her. The way her eyes light up and her breath gets hitchy.

"You gonna take your hair down?" It was phrased like a question, but the implication is more nuanced. Left unsaid was, "Or do I need to do it myself?" But would he?

The battle of wills between them is interesting to watch. The sexual tension molasses thick. I've never seen him this way with a woman, never been around him when he does whatever it is he does that make them swoon. He likes control. Always has. Likes a girl to surrender to him.

Me? I just like sex dirty and messy. I'm easy to please. But watching Bliss and Wylder go head to head over whether or not her ponytail is coming out is somehow making me hard. Would he tie *her* to his bedposts? Would she like to be open and vulnerable to him, trust him that way?

"I prefer my hair up right now," Bliss tells him in a bratty tone. Is she doing that on purpose?

"That's fine. I don't mind you having opinions."

"Oh, aren't you indulgent?" she scoffs.

"I can be, kitten. Especially when I'm happy. And what would make me happy right now is to see all that pretty hair loose on your shoulders."

She studies him. Hell, I study him. If I had a scrunchie, I'd have probably whipped it out of my hair by now. What kind of black magic does my best friend possess? I tip back my glass and watch as Bliss narrows her eyes but reaches out and tugs on the fabric holding her hair up. The long dark waves tumble down even as her eyes flash with annoyance.

"Good girl," Wylder said. "I'll get us some more beer."

Bliss

I DON'T KNOW WHAT JUST happened.

I catch the laughter in Colt's eyes when my hand goes to the ends of my hair. "Why did he do that?"

And why did my insides get all melty from the "good girl" comment?

"You really do have pretty hair."

I close my eyes, my version of burying my head in the sand. "He just likes messing with me."

"I think it's more than that."

My eyes fly open and Colt is looking at me, more serious now. Arousal whooshes through me. Again. Still. I blink. He said something I need to respond to. "Right. More than that."

"Bliss, he likes you. And your hair is pretty."

"He likes to make me nervous is what he likes."

"That's how he is. With women. Women that he likes."

Maybe I shouldn't drink any more beer tonight because I'm having problems tracking this conversation. "What do you mean?"

He looks over his shoulder to check where Wylder is. "He likes to be in control."

"He likes to be a stern, demanding, grumpy Neanderthal is what I think you're trying to say. Should I be impressed that it's all women and not just me?"

"It's not all women. And really, that's not how he sees himself, even if that's how he comes off at first. He thinks women should be protected. Cherished."

I fold my arms across my chest and do an impression of him, lowering my voice. "Ordered around."

Colt laughs. "Yeah, some of that too." The music changes from some kind of death metal to a slow ballad, of all things. "Wanna dance?"

"Oh," I answer, very smoothly. Not. "Um." I'm so verbose. "You want to dance with me?"

He stands and I can't help but follow the movement, sure my eyes are bugging out. He's really got the best body. The way he fills out his jeans make me quiver deep inside. "Yes, I want to dance with you, Miss Camden."

Grasping my hand, he tugs me up and over to the dance floor where there are only two other couples. He pulls me against his muscular frame, one hand firm at my lower back. Holding me in place. I reach my hands up, resting them on his massive shoulders. Where we're pressed tight, I can feel him harden, and I blush, immediately reminded of seeing him in his intimate moment.

"You're blushing, Bliss."

I bite my lip. "I do that a lot. Not sure if you've noticed."

"Oh, I've noticed, darlin'. I notice everything about you lately." He reaches one hand up to stroke my cheek. "I was wondering how that makes you feel?"

I can't concentrate, the nearness of him is way more intoxicating than the beer. "I don't know," I answer truthfully. "I'm not really used to being noticed." I've worked so hard to go unnoticed all these years. It's shocking to hear I haven't slipped under his radar. Or, if I'm to believe him, that of his best friend.

"Do I scare you. Like the others?"

I shake my head. "Oh, no. I promise. I'm not afraid of you. I just...don't know what to do with you." I slap one hand over my mouth. "That sounded weird. Sorry."

He laughs. "You can do anything you want with me." He adds, "Or nothing at all. I just wanted to put it out there that I'm interested. But you're in the driver's seat. With both of us."

I rear my head back and peer all the way up at him. "Both of you?"

I feel a third hand on me, resting lightly on my waist, and a low voice talks directly into my ear from behind me. "You don't have to choose, kitten."

ALL AT ONCE

Chapter Six

Wylder

An hour later, we're at home.

Earlier, Bliss excused herself from the dance floor stuttering about the ladies' room after two minutes of heaven. The scent of her shampoo in my nose while making eye contact with Colt packed an unexpected punch, and my body is still revved and ready for the possibilities. But now we're in the kitchen and nobody knows what to say or do. And all I can think about was how she felt between us.

I'm not a man who is shy about sex or telling a woman what I want. But this arrangement is very different from anything I've ever done. The women that Colt dates are fun party girls who might like more than one night but know going into it with him he isn't looking for more. I scratch an itch occasionally, a lot less than Colt does, but I've never invested more than a night or two, either.

This is new. The woman we both want is not going away the morning after. She's under our protection, as a matter of fact. And if she has any experience, it's not much. Certainly not two older men at once. And after two minutes with her between us at the bar, I already know if this is going to happen, it's going to be both of us together. No trading of rooms and custody agreements about holidays. A woman is the only thing Colt and I have never shared, the thought never even occurring to me before, but instinct tells me that's the way we go forward with Bliss. If we go forward at all.

She's got issues that should stop me cold. She could sue us for harassment if she changes her mind. There is every reason to stop and none to go forward other than I can think of nothing else.

Bliss is moving around the kitchen methodically as she starts a pot of coffee and pulls out some leftover pie. I don't think anyone is hungry, but I know she needs this time in her kitchen to center herself.

Her kitchen? Fuck me, when did I decide this was her kitchen. In my house?

Colt clears his throat and we all snap our attention in his direction. "Are you freaking out, Bliss? You don't have to freak out. You don't even have to say how you feel tonight. We just wanted to let you know we're interested in dating you."

Her lips disappear into each other she's got her jaw so tight. "Both of you want to date me," she reiterates, going back to concentrating on the coffee pot.

"Yes," we both answer.

She stops. "And if I say I don't want to date either of you, I don't have to?"

"Of course not," I answer. "What the fuck kind of question is that?" My heart is racing, and I realize it's in horror. Horror that she thinks either of us would force her.

She rounds on me, pointing the lid to the sugar bowl at me menacingly. "Don't you swear at me, Wylder."

She's right. "I'm sorry I swore at you. I'd hoped you knew us both enough to know that we'd never, ever take away your choice. I don't like to think about why you assume we would."

My apology seems to have surprised her even more than the idea of both of us dating her does. Colt takes the lid from her hands gently. "There is a better way to approach this than we have, I'm sure. But Wylder and I talked about this yesterday."

"You did?"

He looks at me for help, but he's already stepped in it. Nothing I can do now but help him scrape his boot when he's done screwing up. "And well, tonight, hearing the shower stuff pushed my timeline forward a little."

Her shoes scuffing on the kitchen floor suddenly need all her attention. I bring her gaze up to mine with a finger under her chin. "You have all the power here, kitten."

She wants to scoff at that, but realizes she's standing between us again, like on the dance floor, the only place we are touching her is my finger under her chin. The room is thick with uncertainty and awkwardness. Usually, it would be Colt that would smooth things over, make things comfortable again. This time, I think it's up to me.

I let my tone deepen. "How are you feeling, kitten?"

She blinks. "Delightfully terrified, honestly."

The knot of desire in my belly tightens. Need burns and twists through me. I'm not used to the feeling. "What do you want?"

"I don't know?"

"How about this then...what do you need?"

Bliss

NOBODY HAS EVER ASKED me what I want or need before. Nobody. And now I'm sandwiched between the two hottest men I've ever seen for the second time in one night, and my needs and wants are pretty basic.

I might be shy and awkward, but I'm not stupid. "I need you. Both of you." The words tumble out with no finesse at all, but sometimes the truth is raw.

They make eye contact over my shoulder. The sensation of being surrounded is intense. Caged in men. Men who want me, but don't scare me.

"We're gonna take this slow," Colt says, moving the hair off one of my shoulders and pressing a soft kiss to the curve that meets my neck.

I shiver. "Wait. Slow? Why?"

"There's no rush."

"Actually, there might be." I may not be stupid, but I *am* an overthinker. If given the opportunity, I will ruin my chance at a once-in-a-lifetime opportunity to learn about sex from two handsome, virile, gentle yet sexy beasts. "Tonight is good."

"You've been drinking," Wylder points out, his hand on the dip of my waist.

"And we said 'date.'"

If there was enough room for me to stomp my foot, I would. "I thought that was a euphemism."

Wylder's voice rumbles in my ears. "Oh, we're gonna fuck, too, kitten. But not tonight."

I gasp at the word *fuck*. Am I really going to do this? With both of them?

He bends down and kisses me impatiently, shamelessly, pushing me harder into Colt's body. Wylder wraps his hand around my neck like he owns me. His other hand roughly squeezes my breast, and I inhale sharply. Colt's hand slides down my waist, my hip, my thigh, and he murmurs something I can't hear. Something meant to soothe me, I think.

Wylder's force increases, and I moan softly. He pulls back, releasing me. "You need to be sure." He walks away and I slump into Colt. I couldn't stand on my own if I wanted. My entire body is made of gelatin now.

I catch my breath for a few seconds. "Why do you want to date me, Colt?"

His arm tightens around my middle, and he secures me to his chest. "I believe my words to Wylder the other day were about courting."

Courting sounds sweeter than dating. Is that what I want? And that didn't answer my question anyway.

It should be obvious to me that it's more a matter of convenience than anything else, right? They already told me their plans to hire a wife, I guess it got downgraded to dating. It doesn't bother me as much as it should.

They're convenient for me too, right? Two hot men who treat me well isn't the worst way to spend a summer. A lot of girls got their experience earlier in life with earnest high school boyfriends if they were lucky, jerks who used them if they weren't. Colt and Wylder are sexy and experienced. I have no doubt they are good lovers. When I go back to school in the fall, I could be a new woman. Confident.

I just have to make sure I remember it's all temporary. It would be too easy to let my heart get involved.

Colt turns me around, letting go of me except for my wrist. He holds it gently while one callused finger swirls over the delicate skin there in light circles. I've never been so aware of my wrist before. How the pulse skitters in my veins. "Do you hate us? Have we put you off men completely by suggesting this?"

"What? No. I don't think I could ever hate you. You're so good to me. Kinder than I deserve."

"That's where you're wrong, Bliss. You deserve to be treated like a queen." He brings my wrist to his lips and presses the softest kiss to it. "I know it's not conventional, dating two men at once."

"We're not really talking about dating though, are we?"

"There's no rush—"

"I've never had sex before," I blurt out.

"I kinda figured that. There's really no rush. Things will work themselves out the way they're meant."

"I want to. Have sex. With you. And Wylder. I want...I want you both to teach me the things I don't know. And I know I'm blushing horribly right now, and I can't believe I'm saying these things because I'm so shy most of the time."

"I don't think your blush is horrible. I like it." He licks my wrist and my knees turn to jelly. Again. "We don't want you to be scared. We can take our time."

"What if I don't want to take it slow?"

"I guess you're going to have to find a way to convince us you're ready, aren't you?"

He doesn't kiss me hard like Wylder did. He doesn't hold my throat or push his tongue into my mouth roughly. Instead, he cups my cheeks like I'm the most precious thing in the world to him and whispers a soft kiss on the corner of my mouth before leaving me in the kitchen barely able to stand.

Chapter Seven

Colt

The next day is Sunday and we plan a little something special for Bliss after the morning chores are done.

"I really don't think this is a good idea, guys," she says, standing in front of the saddled mare. "I've never been this close to a horse before, much less ridden one."

The look on her face is priceless. This girl has roped me but good.

"We'll keep you safe, sweetheart," I tell her. I get her situated and watch her make a couple of false starts once she gets her foot in the stirrup. I can't help but notice the fiery look in Wylder's eyes as he watches her ass. It's hard not to grab it, I know. I'm fighting it, too.

Once she's in place, I plant myself in the saddle behind her.

"You're riding with me?"

"Best way to learn, Bliss." I lean forward to put my hands around hers above the reins. I press my chest to her back and my chin on her shoulder. "Now squeeze your legs, darlin'."

She shivers at my voice in her ear. At the words that sound so provocative. Fuck, she's going to be so responsive in bed. I just know it.

"You're gonna love learning to ride, kitten," Wylder says and takes off ahead on the trail while I spend some time showing her how to use the reins and her body to control the horse.

I love surrounding her with my body, keeping her safe. I know she says she wants us to teach her about sex, and frankly, that's pretty much all I can think about most of the time, but I don't want to push her. I want her to feel safe and secure with us. I could tell last night she thinks it's a summer fling. And Wylder probably does, too. But me, I'm setting up a foundation for something that will last. Starting with a day in the sun with no expectations other than relax and enjoy the most beautiful place on Earth.

If she can find a measure of peace and joy here, the way I have, maybe she'll want to stay. The situation is unique, and I can't say that I ever thought I'd want to share a woman before. The more I think about what it would be like for the three of us to be happy together, the more I know it won't be trading bedrooms every other night. Not after the two minutes of her between us on the dance floor at the Hound. Not when I realized what it would be like to look into Wylder's eyes when we take her. It has to be together. There was something so right, so electric, last night.

I only have a couple months to convince them both it's worth fighting for. That some people go their whole lives not feeling that spark of rightness.

We stop at the swimming hole, Wylder giving her a hand down, making sure she shimmies down his body before she hits the ground. We brought a bottle of wine and some sandwiches, so I unfold the blanket and get it ready while he shows her the water. We're both dreaming of some skinny dipping today, though neither of us said it in so many words. The words we did exchange this morning in the milking barn were me telling him what she said after he left the kitchen. Him getting a faraway look in his eye and thinking it was too good to be true, and me convincing him it was worth a try.

We're sitting on the blanket in the shade, Wylder with his back against the tree trunk, when Bliss asks, "You guys sometimes talk about the old ranch like it's gone. What happened to it?"

I catch cold fury in Wylder's eyes before he tamps it down. "Nothing you need to be concerned about."

She flinches like he hit her. "I'm sorry."

Hell, the day just got about forty degrees colder.

Wylder closes his eyes. "It's just not really a first date story."

"Second date," I remind them both.

"It's okay. You don't have to tell me."

I don't want to shut this fine day down. He's right, it's not a dating story, but he hides his pain too much. "She should know." It might explain why he's such a grumpy ass sometimes. He doesn't talk about it, he hardly ever did. And only ever with me. I wonder if it'd be good for him to open up to someone else.

Wylder glares at me like he knows what I'm thinking. "It burned down," he says, his voice dipped in the crispy frost of a first freeze.

She bites her lip and looks to me for courage. "It's okay, Wylder. You don't have to tell me."

I put my hand on her shoulder, trying to tell her it's not her that's causing a problem. I'm shocked when Wylder speaks. "My sister married a psychopath. He hit her. A lot. And when she got pregnant, she ran home to the ranch. My parents took her in, of course, thinking she'd be safe."

I close my eyes, trying not to go too deep into the pain with him. They were my family, too. They took me in and treated me like a son. Maybe it's a bad idea to talk about it here, now. I wanted this day to be different. Uncomplicated and fun.

Bliss gets on her knees and takes Wylder's hand, clutching it to her chest. "You don't have to finish the story. I can see it hurts."

His gaze is unfocused, pointed somewhere over the horizon. "He came to the ranch and he shot everyone in the house before he set it on fire."

Bliss loses all color in her face and gasps. "Were you there?"

He rubs the scar on his shoulder, the one where the bullet went in. I answer for him. "He almost bled out." I was in town, trying to get into Lacey June's tight Daisy Dukes while my best friend lay dying. "Everyone in the house died except for Wylder."

But part of him died that day. He's never been the same. Maybe he never will be. I just hold the space for him in case he returns someday.

"Oh my God." Bliss wraps herself around his stiff body like she can shield him from the bullets of the past. "I'm so sorry. What happened to the shooter?"

"Everyone in the house died but me," he says, not melting in her arms, but not pushing her off him either.

"How did he die?"

"I killed him."

Bliss

HE SAYS THE WORDS WITH no emotion, but I can see the turmoil beneath the surface of his eyes. "You killed him?"

Every time I think his story can't gut me more, his words plunge the knife in further. I squeeze him harder, trying to hold him together even though I feel like I could be the one falling apart.

"He was trying to run out after he set the fire, but I woke up enough to wrestle him to the floor."

I'm still confused, but Wylder goes someplace deep and dark inside his mind. "I came home in time to hear the third shot. That woulda been my sister. She was already dead when I got up there. My parents, too. In their own bed, he shot them. I found him pouring gas in the living room, and he shot me. I went down hard, passed out, but came to in time to pull him to the floor before he could flee. I killed him with his own gun. I never saw a man die before, and I'm the one that did it."

My heart starts pounding in my ears.

"It was self-defense," Colt says, trying to buffer my reaction to Wylder as always.

"The hell it was," Wylder replies. "I took his life. I still remember how sick I felt doing it, but it didn't stop me. I'm a monster just as much as he was.."

I don't know what to say or do or even how to feel, but then I look at Wylder's face and things become more clear. I lower from my knees to my backside and pull him into me, cradling his head to my breast as I soothe his soft hair, rocking gently. I'm surprised by his vulnerability. His tense body eventually loosens, his arms coming around me, and he exhales a long, ragged breath. I make eye contact with Colt, and he tucks a tendril of hair that's broken free of my ponytail back behind my ear.

In all my life, nobody has ever needed comforting from me. It's a strange feeling that comes from my heart first and spreads to my limbs. Like I could pass it from me to him just by holding him.

We stay like that for a while until Wylder starts coming back to the present. "Thank you, little one," he tells me and that feeling just explodes in every cell of my body.

Is this what love feels like? When you're warm and fuzzy and wish you could take away someone's pain even if it means you bring it into yourself? That's not a very good thing to feel for a summer fling, is it?

But I do wish I could take it into myself. I wish that Wylder could be the man he was before that night, the man that Colt knows is in there, too. I wish that somehow he could need me, not just want me.

We disentangle after a few more minutes. Small talk injects itself into our conversation to ease away the awkwardness. Even if it's only temporary.

I like these men, I realize as we joke together. As we loosen up so that even Wylder loses some of his stern countenance.

"We're losing the shade," I say as the sun beats down on us.

"Let's go swimming," Colt suggests.

I suppose I knew it was coming when we stopped so close to their swimming hole. Colt stands and offers me a hand up. "I didn't bring a suit," I say, making sure the cliché is completed in the right order.

"I know you didn't." He pulls his shirt over his head, revealing the body of a god. If I start drooling, I will be so embarrassed. "You were

ALL AT ONCE 57

pretty brave in the kitchen last night. How are you feeling in the light of day?"

Honestly, last night and right now seem light years apart. I'm shy and uncertain about my body, what I want to let them do to it, but then I look at Wylder and realize he stripped more than naked for me just now, and my hands find the hem of my t-shirt.

Okay. Step one of being brave about my body has commenced as I feel the sun heat the tops of my breasts still encased in my bra.

Colt swipes his hand down my arm. "Turn around, Bliss."

I turn so I'm facing Wylder, who's still on the ground, and shiver as Colt's hands undo my bra from behind. As it falls, Wylder's eyes get big and he stands up, somehow gracefully. They both tower over me, surrounding me, and my skin erupts in goose bumps despite the heat. Wylder removes his shirt and my hand flies right to the puckered scar. His hand grasps my wrist firmly, like he's going to push me away, but something cracks his resolve, and he lets me smooth over the reminder of his pain.

"Let your hair down," he demands, and this time I don't argue. I don't hesitate. I reach up and release my ponytail and watch his pupils widen.

My hands go to the button on my jeans. I can't believe I'm doing this. Getting naked in front of two men. Two perfect specimens of men, when my body is anything but. It's always caused me problems, but the hungry look in Wylder's eyes gives me a jolt of bravery. I'm not saying I'm not scared. I am. But for the first time in my life, underneath the fear is a courage I never felt before I met Colt and Wylder. I grip the waistband of my jeans and slide my hands down. "I'm not much of a swimmer."

"We won't let you drown," Colt tells me, his big hands taking over pulling down my pants while I keep eye contact with his best friend.

"Are you scared yet, kitten?" Wylder cups my face as I lift one leg out of my pants, followed by the other.

"Yes," I answer truthfully. Because there is no other way to be with Wylder.

I hear Colt's pants rustling behind me. Then his arm wraps around my waist, pulling me into his naked body, his dick hard against my ass. "We're only going for a swim. No funny business."

"What?"

Wylder drops his pants in front of me while I try to figure out what Colt means. He smiles a little too evilly at my expression. He's big everywhere. "What Colt is saying is we decided that today is too soon. We're just getting to know each other."

"I see." So they don't want to have sex with me? I'm so confused. "I thought..."

"Soon," he tells me, then scoops me up and starts walking to the water.

"Put me down. What are you doing?"

He stalks right in with no pause, the water ice cold and shocking. Colt hollers and hoots before he dives in, and suddenly all the tension is gone. They're like boys without a care in the world. They laugh and dunk each other, dunk me, and I forget after a time that I'm naked and just play in a way I don't think I ever had a chance to as a child.

Chapter Eight

Bliss

It's been three days. Three days of torture and longing and an endless ache between my legs. Instead of teaching me all about sex, we watch baseball, we play cribbage, we drink lemonade on the porch and watch the sun go down. We talk about everything and nothing.

But no one lays a hand on me. No one. No, I take that back. I get shoulder squeezes. Hair pats. Even a high five once from Colt. But nothing sexual.

Do they not understand I have needs? They opened a Pandora's box, let me peek into it, then friend-zoned me. Enough is enough. We've seen each other naked. We've kissed. I watched Colt come. And they have stated for the record that they want to do me this summer.

What is the holdup?

I never thought I'd be aching for sex. I never thought I'd be the one to instigate it. But they've pushed me past my limit. I'm going to have to buck up and seduce them myself.

They're in the den watching yet another baseball game when I finish taking a shower after dinner. I spend the extra time slathering my skin with lotion, brushing my teeth, tweezing my brows. And when I walk into the den and sit between them on the couch, both their eyes widen.

"Is that my shirt?" Colt asks.

I nod. "I guess I accidentally put it away in my room. I hope you don't mind me wearing it."

He swallows some beer. "No, of course not."

I smile. Usually, I wear baggy sweats or flannel pajama pants in the evenings, but tonight, just Colt's t-shirt which hangs to about mid-thigh. They don't know what's under it yet. But tonight I'm determined they will find out.

"What are you up to?" Wylder asks.

I shrug innocently. "Nothing."

"You're up to something," he says. "I can always tell when you're going to be extra bratty." He looks into my eyes and raises his eyebrows like he expects something from me.

Surrender.

He's not a boy playing a role. He's a man who is dominant with every fiber of his being. And something about that makes me want to please him. I know his kind of control isn't about physical strength or force. It speaks to something deep inside me. I'm perfectly fine with letting him have control when I know exactly how safe I am with these men.

Something I never thought I'd believe. But I do feel safe. Protected. Cherished. And wanted. Despite the lack of action after skinny dipping.

I shrug. "Just came down to spend some time with my guys. So who's winning the game?"

Wilder reaches for the remote. "I'd say you right now, but you're going to have to tell us what game you're playing."

"I'm not playing a game."

"What's going on?" Colt asks.

Part of me hoped just showing up with fewer clothes on was going to be all I had to do. Alas, my job is not yet done. "I'm ready now."

"Ready for what?" Colt asks. "Exactly?"

"You guys said you wanted me. I told you I wanted you to teach me about sex."

Colt sets his beer down. "And you were told you were going to have to convince us you were ready. There is no rush. We're courting."

I roll my eyes. "I'm ready."

"Prove it," Wylder says, calling my bluff. "Otherwise it's just words."

I take a deep breath and bring Colt's hand under my t-shirt to the place I ached for them the most, all the while keeping my eyes on Wylder.

Colt sucks in a breath and then chuckles. "Our housekeeper forgot her panties, Wylder."

"What a naughty housekeeper." Wylder almost growls the words. "Let's see." He flips my t-shirt up, exposing me to both their gazes. "That's a pretty pussy, isn't it Colt?"

"Makes my mouth water just looking at it."

He squeezes my thigh lightly. Anticipation sucks all the air out of my lungs as I wait for him to take it further. His thumb rubs small circles on the inside of my thigh. I want him to move his hand higher to rub those small torturous circles where I really need him.

I'm not sure when I decided that not only was I going to learn about sex from both of them, but both of them at the same time. Probably about the same time they did, though no one has actually voiced the idea. Colt told me things would unfold naturally, and for some reason, that's what seems the most natural.

"Please. I'm ready. Teach me." I pull my scrunchie out before being asked.

"We're not playing a game, Bliss." Wylder strokes his hands down my hair. "We're not a couple of greenhorns here. We're men. Big men. We'll try to be gentle—"

"I don't need you to be gentle. I need you to want me as much as I want you."

"Oh, kitten. You have no idea."

"Is this what you wanted, sweetheart?" Slowly, Colt eases his finger into my pussy, spreading the moisture around.

"Spread your legs," Wylder demands.

When I do, Colt's finger slips inside me. He gently works it in and out, pressing further and further into me with each little thrust.

"She's so wet and tight," he tells Wylder, his voice full of awe.

"Look at me," Wylder commands, and I turn my face to him. "Is this what you wanted? Did your little pussy lead you down here tonight?"

"Yes," I whisper.

"Tell me you want this."

"I want this, Wylder. I *need* this."

"Good girl."

Colt's finger slides back into me. I moan and spread my legs wider. I can't help the heavy breathing and little sounds I'm making.

"You're so responsive," he tells me.

Wylder pulls up my shirt more and slides his hands to my breasts. He groans long and low as he starts squeezing them, pushing them together, running his hands over them.

I gasp, pushing my chests up into his hands, my nipples hard against his palms. The sensations are too much and not enough at the same time.

"Please."

"Please what, darlin'?" Colt asks, adding a second finger, spreading me apart, stretching me.

"I don't know," I say, as Wylder continues squeezing my breasts, pulling on my nipples. "Please don't stop?"

I look up to see Wylder and Colt exchanging a silent message with each other before looking down at me again.

"We won't stop unless you want us to, kitten," Wylder says. Then he kisses me. It's not like the rough kiss in the kitchen. It's slower, fuller. I can feel his longing for me in it and it ratchets up my own desire.

"We can make you feel even better," Colt says when we come up for air. "Would you like that? Are you ready for more? Or do you want to take a break?"

"I'm ready," I answer even though a part of me would love to run out of here and pack my bags and go. But I don't want to be that girl my whole life. I like being this one more. This girl who has somehow caught the interest of two men who can show her pleasure instead of fear.

"Why don't you sit up on Wylder's lap then," Colt suggests, withdrawing his fingers and licking them off, eyes closed.

Something inside me just changes. Like something primal wakes up, looks around, and desires with an intensity I've never felt before. I want dark things. Dirty things. And these men are going to open my whole world up.

My whole life, I've run from men who wanted to use my body. They didn't care about me. They wouldn't have thought twice about hurting me. But tonight, the shift inside me is powerful. It's not weakness to give myself to Colt and Wylder. It's not scary or wrong. They care about me and suddenly I want them to use me. Use my body. I want their focus solely on me. I want to be the center of their world tonight. I want to submit to their desires and lose myself in their passion.

My body isn't a trap anymore. It's the key to unlocking *everything*.

Wylder helps me sit up, removing the shirt as I straddle his lap. He stretches his long legs wide so I'm spread open for the two of them to see. No shame. No hiding.

"You taste delicious," Colt tells me, moving off the couch, "and I can't wait to taste more." He gets down on his knees in front of me. Wylder's hands are back on my breasts, pulling and pushing them together. God, to think I hated my breasts all these years. They feel amazing now.

After sliding his finger in and out of me a few times, Colt holds it up to my lips. "Taste yourself, darlin.'"

My lips open obediently, and his wet fingers slide in. They both moan.

"Such a dirty girl." Wylder says it with such reverence that I'm humbled. Eager to be dirtier.

Wylder grips my breasts tightly in his big hands and Colt spreads me open and takes a big lick, forcing a cry of pleasure from me. Then he really digs in.

"Oh!" I gasp, hips thrusting in Wylder's lap, his hard dick pressing tight against my back.

Of course, I knew about this, even if I never experienced it. I just didn't know that having the right man's tongue there would change my entire world.

"Have you ever had someone eat you out before, kitten?" Wylder's voice in my ear while another man's mouth is on me sends extra shivers through me. This is so wrong it's right. So bad it's good.

"No."

"Mmm. Good. You're ours now. You know that, right?" Wylder asks, bouncing my breasts in his hands. His hands are big, but my breasts overflow them as he squeezes.

"Yes," I gasp out as Colt finds my clit, giving it quick little flicks with his tongue while he slides a finger deep inside me. Then a second. I continue to squirm and gasp as he pumps his fingers in and out.

"Good girl," Wylder growls before kissing and nibbling on my neck, squeezing my nipples hard, the sharp pain going straight to my clit under Colt's tongue.

"So then no one's touched or licked you here either?" asks Colt as his fingers slide out of my pussy and down, circling around my asshole before one finger pushes a little inside.

"No!" I say in shock, not sure how to feel about the fingers playing around there. I clench everything, suddenly uncertain. "Is that...normal?"

"Looks like there are all kinds of things we can teach you," Colt says, bending his head back down. "Isn't that right, Wylder?"

Wylder slides one hand down my stomach to my clit, while the other continues to grip a breast. "We'll teach you all kinds of ways to feel good, kitten. Would you like that?"

Wylder's fingers slide up and down, getting wet, before circling my swollen clit slowly, while Colt continues to finger my asshole gently. This is more than I signed up for. I'm sliding out of my comfort zone until lightning zaps up my spine. I can feel my pussy throb in every nerve of my body. It's all too much..

"Oh, God! Don't stop!"

"That's it, kitten," Wylder whispers in my ear, his fingers going into overtime on my clit. "Come for us, that's a good girl."

My hips keep bucking up to meet Wylder's fingers, while Colt sits back on his heels and watches me writhing on Wylder's lap. When I open my eyes, I see he's brought his dick out of his pants while watching me.

"You know, darlin'," he says, spreading his precum around the head and down the shaft, stroking faster but without the urgency from the other night, "we can teach you how to make us feel good, too. Would you like to learn that tonight?"

I bite my lip as I imagine doing what he's doing right now, stroking his big dick in my hands. I squirm against Wylder's cock, pressing hard under my ass, his rough hands squeezing my breasts and rolling the nipples between his thick fingers. "Yes, I want to do everything with you both."

"That's my good girl," Wylder growls in my ear.

God, I love hearing those words from him. Love knowing I've pleased him somehow.

Colt stands up from his crouch on the floor, dropping his pants and boxers all the way down and off. He pulls his shirt off over his head, and I can see his hard abs, the vee of his hips, and most importantly, his big, thick cock is now jutting out in front of my face.

Hot. Forbidden. And fascinating. I can't stop looking at him, and I really can't wait to put my hands, mouth, lips, teeth, tongue, and the rest of my body all over him. I'm under some kind of sex spell, and I hope to God no one ever breaks the hex.

Colt holds himself in his hand, stroking it as he steps closer to me. He exchanges a look with Wylder behind me, and they must come to some kind of agreement because Colt steps even closer, between Wylder and my spread legs, and aims his dick at my lips.

"Have you ever sucked cock before, Bliss?" Wylder asks me, low in my ear, sending shivers down my back.

I shake my head, looking up at Colt. "No, Wylder," I say quietly. They know I haven't. They're drawing this out. My complete surrender to all of our desires.

While Colt strokes himself with one hand, his other caresses my cheek. "You're so perfect for us, Bliss." I turn my head to press a kiss to his palm, and he smiles down at me.

In all my life, I never equated lust with sweetness. I didn't know that sex could be nurturing and friendly even while it was raw and dirty. But I feel so secure. So necessary and needed and wanted, and I also feel like I want to be used.

He brings the tip back to my lips and starts to rub it gently back and forth across my lips, spreading his precum on them like lip gloss.

"You just relax and let us guide you through this." Wylder adjusts beneath me trying to find some relief I'm sure. "You don't need to worry about a thing."

I nod my head, mesmerized by the feel of the soft skin of Colt's penis against my lips. Wylder presses a kiss to my neck. I feel cherished in the arms of Wylder while Colt looks at me so tenderly. My tongue darts out to taste Colt, and he groans. "Open up for me, Bliss."

I part my lips just enough to have Colt slip the tip of his dick inside. I bring my hands up to his bare thighs, feeling the crisp leg hairs and hard muscle beneath my palms, while I swirl my tongue around to taste more of him. So many textures to enjoy.

"That's it, baby," Colt said. "Get it nice and wet with your tongue."

"Open up a little wider, kitten," Wylder tells me, gently stroking my neck.

I open my mouth wider, letting more of Colt into my mouth. I'm stretched wide, but there's so much more of him left.

"You're doing great, darlin'," Colt says, both of his hands slipping around my head to bury themselves in my hair.

He pulls out of my mouth a little bit, and then thrusts back in while bringing my head forward. His dick feels huge in my mouth, and I have to breathe through my nose as I suck. Wylder takes my hands and pins them so I'm cupping my own breasts. I might feel more in control of the blow job if I could use my hands, but I'm enjoying the sense of being dominated by both of them. Safe, but theirs to play with.

"That's it," Wylder whispers in my ear. "You're such a good girl, sucking Colt's big dick. Keep sucking, baby. Let him fuck your mouth."

Wylder tilts my chin up at a different angle, while Colt starts to thrust in and out of my mouth faster and harder.

"You're doing so good. You feel amazing, Bliss," Colt tells me, continuing to pull my head farther onto his dick.

I start to gag as he hits the back of my throat. "Good job, kitten," Wylder tells me, pulling me off to catch my breath. "Do you think you're ready to have Colt come in your mouth?"

I would do just about anything to please these men. Anything they ask. Anything they want. I'm not in control of my body, but more me than I've ever felt before. None of it makes sense, but it doesn't have to.

"I think so," I say, looking up at Colt nervously, while he strokes his dick, bringing it back to press against my lips.

I open my mouth and he slides back in. Colt's hands fist in my hair as he moves his hips back and forth, deeper with each thrust.

"That's it, baby," Wylder encourages me, one hand back on my clit. "Play with your nipples. You're being such a good girl, and you're going to get such a big reward when he comes in your mouth."

I feel like a right good slut. In the best way possible. I can't believe this is happening.

"Can you swallow for me, darlin'?" Colt asks, his words coming out in gasps as his dick hits the back of my throat.

I try to answer around his dick, and the vibrations must feel good because he throws his head back with a groan, giving a few short, hard thrusts of his hips, and starts to come in my mouth. It hits the back of my throat in thick and salty spurts. I swallow, and then he pulls out with enough time to come a little more on my chin.

"Jesus Christ, Bliss," Colt says, breathing hard, staring down at me, his hands having left my hair but now cupping my cheeks while we gaze at each other. "Jesus Christ, that was amazing."

Wylder grunts. I turn on his lap, his eyes meet mine and his tongue dives into my mouth, tasting me, tasting Colt.

And I'm ready for my education to continue.

Chapter Nine

Wylder

Her lips are soft and pillowy, and knowing I also taste my best friend on her tongue drives up my desire. I kiss her hungrily, swallowing her whimpers. I've heard her come now, and I want to hear it again. And again. She kisses me back, gripping me desperately with her hands fisting my shirt. Jesus, I'm still clothed and everyone else is naked.

"Are you ready for more, kitten, or do you need a break? We can start again tomorrow."

She blinks in surprise, looking at me, then Colt, then back at me. "But you haven't..."

"I'll be fine. I don't want you to have any regrets. We've got all summer." Every single word physically hurts as it comes out of my mouth. But I can beat off tonight if she needs more time. I've got plenty of new material since I held her when she came and while she was blowing my best friend.

She turns in my arms so she's sitting sideways on my lap instead of backwards astride. "I don't intend to wake up a virgin in the morning."

That's my brave girl.

I put one leg under her knees and stand with her in my arms. "Then let's go take care of you some more."

Her arms loop around my neck. "Where are we going?"

"You're not losing your virginity on the couch."

"So only oral on the couch?"

Colt laughs as he follows us up the stairs. "We can fuck on the couch plenty. Just not your first time."

I set her in the middle of her bed. "Scoot up and spread your legs."

The cute little thing blushes. After all she's already done, she blushes.

I pull off my shirt and her eyes get big. Then they get even bigger when I lower my pants. "Spread your legs. I shouldn't have to tell you twice."

She huffs out an indignant breath but does it.

"Here in bed," I say darkly, my voice deep and low, "I own you."

She nods, a little mesmerized, I think.

"What do you think, Colt?"

"She's beautiful. Wait till you taste her for yourself."

I wedge myself between her thighs, grinding my cock into her wet mound. I lean down and kiss her as I line up with her wet folds. She gasps into my mouth as I rock my hips, sliding up and down, coating my cock with her slick juices. I take it slow, though it kills me, pushing my cock up until it rubs against her clit, and then back down to tease her entrance. She squirms under me, moaning and getting wet enough to leave a spot on the bed. I take her hands and pin them down to either side of her head, holding her there as I go faster and faster, grinding my hips into her clit whenever I get the chance. She's close again, but I want to be inside her when she comes.

"Let me help," Colt offers and kneels near her, restraining her wrists.

Fuck, that's so hot. She's pinned down by both of us now.

Carefully, I line up my cock with the entrance and slowly, very slowly, I slide just the head inside her. She is tight.

So tight.

"Look at her take that big dick," Colt says, admiration in his voice.

"This is going to hurt, kitten," I tell her, holding her still. Her eyes widen, both fear and desire painted in them. Her body tenses, her fingernails digging into my skin. I kiss her forehead, trying to smooth the frown, then her eyelids, her cheeks, the tip of her nose, and finally her mouth. She locks on immediately, kissing me back passionately.

I move back, giving her some room and changing the angle, and Colt dives onto her breast sucking so hard I feel the tight squeeze of her pussy in reaction. Oh, she's ready for more. I lift her legs over my shoulders, making her squeak in surprise.

Colt is mauling her tits now. Possessed almost. "Fuck her. Fuck that tight little virgin pussy, Wylder."

His dirty words spur me to quicken the pace, going into her a little harder, our bodies slapping. Hard and fast. She doesn't just lie there. She's clutching Colt to her chest, her fingers tugging his hair, her other hand pinching her own nipple. Fuck. She's perfect for me. For us.

"Come on my cock," I tell her, pounding into her sweet little cunt. It tightens, squeezing me. She's close. Very close.

"You're a dirty little girl. You love it, don't you? You love my thick cock in your little princess pussy. You love your big tit in Colt's mouth. You're a needy little thing, aren't you? So naughty you need two cowboys in your bed." I pinch her clit, maybe too hard. "Come on my cock, baby. Come for me."

On command, she does. She lets out a scream, her body quaking as her pussy contracts around my cock.

I know I should pull out. I absolutely know it. She says she's got an IUD in, but it's my responsibility to take care of her. But then I have a thought of impregnating our shy little housekeeper—and I instantly come, jetting my seed inside her, spurt after spurt, filling her up.

Colt

I'M HARD AS HELL AGAIN. I guess that's the downside of taking turns. The time spent watching the live porn in front of me was enough to recover. But our sweet girl is going to need to rest. It's been a lot for one night.

Wylder eases off her. So much cum. Jesus. I had no idea he had so much stored up in there. He's one virile bastard.

I pull Bliss onto my chest, gathering her close, skin to skin, when he goes to the bathroom. It sounds like he's getting ready to clean her up, so I just hold her, stroking her soft skin. "You doing okay still?"

Please say yes.

"I feel amazing."

The weight on my chest lifts. "We didn't push you too hard? We were a little rough."

"I loved everything we did tonight. I feel so deliciously naughty..." Her voice drifts at the end and she pulls away. The room chills about ten degrees.

"Whoa. What's wrong darlin'?"

She shivers, not the good kind. "I told myself I would never be like my mom." She sits up like she's looking for something to put on. "This is just like something she would do, I think."

"Hey," I say, trying to still her. "There is nothing wrong with a healthy sex life. The things your mom did, her attitude about what she was worth and what you were worth, have nothing to do with what we have."

"Don't they?"

Wylder comes in with a wet towel and narrows his eyes. "What's going on?"

"Bliss is having some regrets."

"No!" she yells. "Not regrets. Not exactly. Not about you guys. You didn't do anything wrong. I'm just...it's just..."

"Lie back, baby," he tells her in a gravelly voice.

And she does. She locks her knees together until he gives her a sharp look, then she relaxes. While he gently cleans her, I pull her back into me, trying to surround her. Make her feel safe. "You are priceless.

Worth more than anything in this world." Damn her mom for making her feel so hunted. Like she had to protect herself from her own body.

She doesn't say anything, but at least she's not arguing.

"We don't want anything but to make you feel good. You can explore anything you want with no judgment from us. It's not weak or bad to have sex. To want sex."

Wylder kisses her bent knee. "It's not weak or bad not to want it, either. You just have to promise to be honest with us about what you need and want. If all we ever have is tonight, that's perfectly fine."

The hell it is. I want to howl. But he's right. She is in control of how far we go and how often.

"Why me?" she asks. "Why are you both so perfect and still you want me? I'm nothing special."

"Don't you ever say that again," Wylder commands. "Nobody insults our girl, and that includes you."

I sit her up gently. "We're not perfect, Bliss. We're just two dumb cowboys who were smart enough to see how special you are."

She reaches up and cups my jaw. She's searching for something. The truth? A lie? I don't know. All I can think about is how perfect she is for us. How this is something so special that I'm afraid we could lose it too easily.

"I think I need to be alone tonight. Is that okay?"

"Of course it's okay. But if you change your mind, we'll hold you all night long."

We leave her, and I go downstairs to get my clothes and turn off all the lights. My heart feels like a rock in my chest. I hear Wylder when I come out of the kitchen. "Hey. I checked all the doors."

He nods but looks oddly out of sorts for Wylder. "You think she's going to be okay?"

"I think she's stronger than she thinks she is. It's not going to be easy earning her trust. She's only going to let go of it a little at a time. We just have to be patient."

"We didn't push her too hard tonight, did we?"

"I hope not."

"She's something else, right?" he asks as I get to the bottom of the stairs.

"Wait till you taste her."

Chapter Ten

Bliss

When I get downstairs this morning, I smell food. Which is impossible since I'm not cooking anything.

I find not one but two cowboys moving around my kitchen, and it looks like they used every dish in it. "Did we have an earthquake?" I ask, taking in the haphazard mess around me. Is that batter on the wall? How did they get batter on the wall?

Colt shifts from one foot to another as he takes in the mess through my eyes. He's wearing one of my aprons. Maybe I'm still dreaming. I mean, all my other dreams were sexual last night, but perhaps this one is just thrown in to be weird. "We were going to make you breakfast in bed."

"You were?"

"But you're here now."

I see Wylder is squeezing oranges and also wearing an apron. This is one messed up dream. "That's really sweet. You remember that making breakfast is my job, right?"

"Don't be sassy and sit down," Wylder tells me.

Instead, I go to the coffee pot first. As I pour, I take in the damage to my workspace. It's going to take me hours to clean this up. "It's really sweet of you to cook for me. Thank you."

They guys look at each other and…Wylder…smiles. Almost sheepishly. I must be dreaming. He's got such a nice smile and I never see it.

But this is real, I think, because if I were dreaming then they'd be naked under the aprons.

As we eat, they very obviously avoid asking me how I'm feeling. Or if I'm doing okay. Or if I'm sore. (The answer to that last is hell, yeah. But it's a nice ache.)

They refuse to let me clean the kitchen. Instead, Colt draws me a bath and they affirm I am to do no housework while they are out today. Instead, I am supposed to rest all day. Like I have a cold or something, I guess.

The thing is, I feel great. I had a little emotional setback last night, but my body feels loose and languid, and the way they spoiled me this morning is the complete opposite of mornings at my mom's house. They are nothing like my mom's boyfriends, and I am nothing like my mom. I get it now.

I actually do try to do some cleaning while they are gone, but I suck up a sock in the vacuum and burn the belt to shit. Also, the washing machine keeps rocking like it's trying to break out of the basement, so I turn it off and unplug it for good measure. I am, possibly, the worst housekeeper ever. So I bake. Letting my mind wander from my ingredients to all the things I learned last night. All the things I still don't know about.

I spend hours baking, losing myself in the process. I will so miss this kitchen come September. I can't even imagine going back to my little apartment that has a microwave and mini-fridge only.

Yes, it's totally this kitchen that I will miss when I leave this fall.

When the guys come in, I'm overwhelmed with strange new feelings. I missed them today. I feel…complete…when we're all in the same room. I am in so much trouble. My heart is toast.

"You okay, Bliss?" Colt asks.

God, he's so sweet. And Wylder isn't naturally as kind, but he cares in his own way. By taking charge, taking responsibility, assuring the kind of consistency and security I never knew growing up. He makes you feel like nothing bad could happen to you if he's in the room, if you're under his wing.

I cross the kitchen and put one hand on each of their chests. "Thank you for today. I'm fine. I'm better than fine. I want to kiss you, but I'm not sure how I'm supposed to make the choice of who first."

"Then I guess it's all for one," Colt says, leaning down and bringing Wylder's head down with him.

Both of their mouths on mine is an affirmation I didn't know I needed. It's sloppy and uncoordinated, and I'm sure they're getting lips and tongue of each other while we kiss, but pieces of my heart click together in a way I didn't know they could. I'm in love with them. Of course, I am. And I'm not going to ruin what time I have with both of them with sadness for the future. I'm taking this happiness while I can. My hands wander down to their growing bulges and they both groan.

"Easy, darlin'. We don't expect sex every time we walk in the door," Colt says.

"Speak for yourself, Hoss," Wylder says.

I laugh. "What about my expectations? Maybe I expect sex every time you walk in the door." I rub their growing erections with a confidence I didn't know I possessed. "I want you both inside me. Can we do that?"

Colt throws his hat onto the hook behind him. "Hell, yes, we can do that."

We shed clothes as we make our way to my bedroom, stopping for kisses and touches of skin as it's exposed. Wylder stops in his room to get lube. But then Colt's tongue is in my mouth and he carries me to the bed.

He nestles between my legs, licking and sucking so gently that I squeeze my thighs around his ears trying to get more friction, squirming against the intense sensations swirling through me.

"Fuck, yeah," comes a deep growl. "Lick her hot little pussy."

Colt lifts his head. "You need to taste her." He shifts and holds my legs open to Wylder.

Oh, wow. I can't believe I'm getting excited by the way they talk like I'm some kind of sex doll, the way they treat me like a plaything.

Wylder wastes no time. His hot tongue licks a long, hot path over my overly sensitive pussy. I grab his hair, tightening my fingers in it, as he licks me deliberately, again and again, swiping his tongue inelegantly and rough, drawing me closer to orgasm only to back off before I go over the edge.

He takes my clit between his lips and sucks on it relentlessly until I shriek. Out of nowhere, Colt sucks on my earlobe, and I start to lose it. Two mouths on me. Four big hands. I am all nerve endings and voltage. Colt cups one of my breasts, rolling my hard nipple between his fingers while I whimper. Wylder is tonguing me deeply now, and as I gasp with pleasure, his fingers begin pinching my swollen clit.

"Yesssss," I moan. This is so dirty, I hardly believe it's me. Like I was made for this.

Wylder growls into my melting center. His hands slide to my ass, squeezing the cheeks roughly and pulling them apart, pinching and massaging my ass and licking me more firmly.

I'm about to come and come hard when he stops.

"But..."

"Get on top of Colt, Bliss," Wylder says gruffly.

"I need..."

"Believe me, kitten. We know exactly what you need."

I let Colt guide me on top of him, centering myself over his cock, my legs braced on either side of his hips. He spreads me open and settles his thick shaft along my quivering center.

"Please," I whisper. I've never been so desperate to come. Colt just tangles his fingers in my hair and pulls me down for a soft kiss. I shudder when he massages his way down my back. Then large hands cup my cheeks from below, squeezing and opening me to Wylder's gaze.

"This is going to be cold," Wylder warns.

"What?"

Cool liquid is suddenly drizzled down the cleft of my butt. He uses his finger to rub it into my sensitive opening. I twist to look over my shoulder, and Wylder is rubbing more lube on himself, fisting his shaft until it glistens. His half-lidded gaze roves over the curves of my ass, and he looks dangerous and feral.

I'm aware of Colt beneath me, but we're all focused on what Wylder is going to do next. He grips my hips, nudging himself against my opening. I tense up, of course. This feels pretty momentous. Maybe too momentous. I have to remember this was my idea.

Wylder leans close, his warm breath on my ear, and the heat from his chest beating onto my bare back.

"You're beautiful, Bliss." His voice is soft. Low. My whole body flushes at the compliment. He pushes in, just a little, but my narrow channel spasms around his thickness. I gasp when he pushes further.

I groan, burying my face in Colt's neck. It hurts. Wylder feels enormous back there. I can't possibly take any more.

"You're perfect," Wylder breathes in my ear.

Okay, I'm far from perfect, but his words have a magical effect. My whole body relaxes, opening to him.

"Yes," he whispers. "That's it. That's right."

Sensations beyond anything I've ever imagined flood my body. Colt's patient fingers stroke me in front, his other hand warm and secure on my thigh. Colt's thick shaft at my center is reassuring, somehow. I'm pinned in place, open to both of them. There isn't any way for me to hide.

My whole body trembles with arousal. With a little bit of humiliation that heightens my pleasure. This may have been my idea, but I've let go of any control I might have had, ceding it to them, and trusting we'll all make it out alive.

"I'm ready," I whisper. Wylder lets out a hissing groan, sinking into me all the way. I feel every twitch of his hot cock. Everything is all so incredibly hot and intense and overwhelming.

And then Wylder moves my hips, and Colt's thick head is at my pussy entrance.

"You can't both fit—" I gasp. "I know I asked for this, but I'm already so full."

"You can do this, Bliss." Colt's kisses are so coaxing that I get lost in them until he slides all the way in.

I'm holding them both in my body, and we all pause.

"Jesus. You feel so amazing." Wylder groans.

I'm crowded between them, full. Beyond full. I have no more choices, and I don't want any. I just give into the sensations.

Wylder lengthens his strokes. All I can do is give in to his strong body driving against mine. Colt whispers reassurances in my ear as Wylder begins to fuck me in earnest. Colt starts moving, too, thrusting up when Wylder moves back. Every one of their movements ripples through my body.

"Wylder, man, I can feel the veins in your dick. This is wild."

Sparks of pleasure dance behind my eyes. We're joined so intimately, so obscenely. From behind, Wylder's muscular arm presses against my hip, his hand cupping my mound just above Colt's cock. His fingers caress my clit and my body clamps down on both of them, knowing that they can feel each other, that Wylder's hand must be bumping into Colt.

"Fucking come right now, Bliss," Wylder demands.

I have no choice. Their cocks just keep sawing in and out, nudging up the wave of my orgasm that spills over when Wylder pinches my clit hard.

"God, oh God, oh God..." I shake through an orgasm that just won't stop. The pleasure is overwhelming, almost painfully so.

Animal growls from both men fill the room, bouncing off the walls like we're in a cave. We're one animal now.

Colt's gaze is focused over my shoulder on Wylder, and that's when Wylder's arm comes around and cups the back of Colt's head roughly.

They're close enough to kiss, and the intensity between them feels so rough and raw and perfect. This moment isn't about them sharing me. It's us. The three of us. As one.

Wylder's cock twitches against my tight ring of muscles. "Gonna fucking fill you up." Hot cum spurts into me, and I swear I feel every splash. Colt grasps both my hips firmly, thrusting long and hard into me, and he too fills me, his deep groans so primal.

We are one sweaty body, joined together, barely able to breathe, and everything is different now.

Chapter Eleven

Wylder

I wake up in an angel's bed, my mind flooded instantly with memories from the hottest, most intense night of my life. There were a few minutes when the three of us were one. I've never felt anything like it. I was fucking them both. They were both fucking me. It wasn't something normal. Or ordinary. I roll closer so I can spoon Bliss, running a slow hand down her...bumpy abs. I pull my hand away and sit up at the same time as a very shocked Colt.

Holy shit. We stare at each other for a few minutes, and he cracks a smile. "Awkward."

My hand feels hot, like it's blushing. I didn't think hands blushed.

And touching Colt just now stirred up the memory of looking into his eyes when we were connected inside Bliss. My dick might not have been inside him, but I was inside him all the same. And now I have to say something.

"Sorry. I thought Bliss was still in the middle. Where is she?"

"Standing in the doorway watching you two freak out."

We turn our heads to the door of her bathroom. She's wearing Colt's t-shirt and a bemused smile.

"Nobody's freaking out," Colt says calmly. He asks me, "Are we?"

"I don't freak out," I answer gruffly, trying to find my center. I've never woken up naked in bed with a man before. This is weird, but something we need to get used to if we are going to keep doing this for the rest of the summer.

"So, if you're not freaking out, touch him again," she says.

"What?" Colt asks, pulling up the sheet.

She crosses the room and sits on the edge of the bed like she wants to watch a show. She's daring me. What's her game here? "If we're going to continue this affair, there is going to be accidental touching more often than not considering the close quarters. Friendly fire..." she smiles evilly. "Crossing swords..."

"Yes, *accidental*," Colt affirms.

"What are you up to?" I ask her. "And don't tell me nothing. I can see the wheels turning in your head."

She folds her knees up under her. "It seems to me that I've been asked to be the most vulnerable every time. To spread myself open to you both and trust. Which I do, now. I trust you both. And I'm glad you were there for my first time, but why can't you be vulnerable, too? Are you afraid you'll be gay if you touch each other on purpose?"

Colt rubs his face like he's trying to wake up. This conversation is a little much before coffee. "Are you asking if we're homophobes, darlin'? We're not. We just aren't attracted to each other that way."

She's still daring me with her eyes. I narrow mine right back. "Life would have been a lot simpler for us if we were gay. We've lived in the same house all these years. I can't believe we never thought about it. Think of all the sex we could have been having, Colt."

"Shut up, Wylder."

She takes the scrunchie off her wrist and very deliberately scoops her hair into a messy bun while watching my expression. "Well, if you're not afraid of being gay, then you must be afraid of being vulnerable in front of me. Which isn't fair. I have to touch both of you."

"Oh, you *have* to touch both of us?" Colt grabs hold of her shirt and pulls her up to where we are. "Such a hardship for you, I suppose."

She giggles. It's the first time I've heard it. She's happy here. With us. She's comfortable in this bed—no hiding, no stammering. *We've made her happy.*

Everything in my life is different now, hearing that giggle. Shit. I didn't want my life to change. I don't want or need more to care about than I do. She's too young for us. She's got big plans. But I'm in love with her. And fuck if that doesn't scare me.

"Where'd you just go, Wylder?" she asks. "It looks like a trip to Serioustown over there. Does it bother you that much?"

"If touching my damned best friend will make you happy, I'll do it. I'm not worried about my manhood, kitten. Are you?"

"Do I get a say here?" Colt asks.

I ignore him. "Just let's get it over with. Where do you want me to touch him?"

"I'd really like a say," Colt protests.

She bites her lip and peruses his body thoughtfully. "His torso is fine."

"Do I need to look deeply into his eyes while I'm doing it?"

She giggles again. That's a really nice sound. "No. You're really going to do it?"

I reach over her and put my hand out, but stop an inch away from contact with him. I don't know why this is all of the sudden such a big deal. I swallow around the tennis ball in my throat, place my hand on his bare chest over his heart, and we both exhale. I can feel the increase in his heartbeat, the crinkle of his chest hair, but all I hear is the roar of my own blood. Bliss puts her hand near mine, then slowly brings it down, caressing over those bumpy abs I grazed earlier.

Colt is holding his jaw so tight, but he's not pulling away. Without any real thought, my hand begins moving, and I trace the outline of one of his pecs, the hardness of muscle beneath smooth skin intrigues me. My fingers accidentally skate across a nipple and the sensation makes him moan.

Interesting.

He's being stoic, and I can't read him at all. I like it better when I know what he's thinking. I pinch the tightened nipple before allowing my flat palm to coast down his abs.

"Fuck, Wylder."

I can feel the trail of hair that begins below his belly button, and the awareness of his body is so new. I make the mistake of looking deeply into his eyes after all. His pupils are blown. I could write it off that Bliss is touching him, too, but there's an intensity to our connection. He sits up, the sheet pooling around his lap.

I'm stuck in that moment right before the jack-in-the-box pops out. That second your feet hit the diving board, but you're not yet airborne. I know something is coming and that is going to scare me even though I know it's coming. Adrenaline rushes through me, but it won't prepare me. Not for this.

Then his lips are on mine. They are surprisingly soft, full. Not like a woman's, firmer. I cup his jaw with one hand, the sensation of his morning stubble a new one for my palm. Our breathing is fast and ragged. God, we're naked in a bed and my tongue is in my best friend's mouth.

Bliss has her hand in the hair at the back of my head like she's trying to keep me there. It hasn't occurred to me to stop kissing him. It feels so good. Different from what I'm used to, but so damn good. His masculine energy is almost battling mine. Kissing a woman has always felt like a give and take, but kissing Colt is both of us taking and neither of us giving.

He pulls back first. "What is happening?"

Before I can answer, Bliss does. "Nothing that you don't want to happen. Don't get me wrong, this is so hot. Hotter than I ever thought it could be. But I don't expect you guys to keep going just to please me. Consent works for all of us the same, right?"

My dick is hard from kissing my best friend. Really hard. My thoughts race, trying to find a track that makes sense. There isn't one.

"We've got work to do," I say, pretending I'm back in asshole mode. "We can talk about this later."

I go to my own room and take a shower, try to clear my head. But it won't clear. I can't settle on one thought before another takes its place.

Last night was my first threesome. I realized I'm in love with Bliss this morning. My best friend kissed me, and I wanted more.

It's all too much, and I regret like hell that I didn't fire Bliss Camden that first time I saw her in the kitchen and knew she was trouble. I'm out of control, and I don't know how to deal with being out of control.

I lied the night I told Bliss I liked my demons just fine. The only other time in my life when I couldn't control my world, after I lost my family and murdered a man, I almost didn't make it out of that depression. All this time, I've been keeping my demons at bay by not feeling anything too much, by not needing anything too much.

But the demons are awake now, aren't they?

When I come out of the bathroom, Colt is standing in my room like a reversal of the night Bliss and I watched him come in his shower.

My stomach is flipping all over itself, and I grasp the towel around my waist tightly. "What are you doing in here, Colt?"

"Later is now."

Colt

WYLDER IS NOT HAPPY. But that "we'll talk later" he left me with is a bunch of bullshit. So later is now.

He brushes past me to his dresser. "In case you forgot, we have a ranch to run. Our love life is gonna have to wait."

"Love life, huh? I was here to talk about our sex life, but if you're in love with me now, I can hardly blame you. I'm quite the catch."

He shoots me a look while he rifles through his dresser, pulling out clothes and throwing them on his bed. "We're not doing this now."

"Actually, we are. We have to. This ain't the kind of thing you let fester."

I know people don't understand Wylder, sometimes. I see through him. I always have. How he acts gruff when he isn't. He's the most belligerently domineering when he's feeling most out of control.

"So we kissed. Big deal. Now we have to go check fences. There. Talk done."

Oh, he's really out of sorts. Can't blame him. I've got no idea what happened to us both in the last twenty-four hours. Bliss is the one who lost her virginity, but she's better than fine. Apparently, Wylder and I get to be the emotional ones about everything.

"Wylder, you're my best friend. Don't shut me out."

He looks like he wants to throw me physically out of this room. "What do you want me to say?"

"How do you feel? Are you disgusted with me?"

That changes the angry look on his face to one of concern. "Disgusted? Why would I be disgusted with you?"

"Well, you ran out so fast. What was I supposed to think?"

God damn, but he's a big dude. I'm not sure why I'm just noticing that now. I'm not sure about a lot of things.

A wave of different emotions ebb and recede over his face. Confusion, anger, regret. "We crossed a line. I'm not sure it was a good idea, but I'm not disgusted by you. I just wasn't prepared for that to happen. And if things don't work out, I don't want it to come between us."

I feel like I can breathe for the first time since he touched me. It was probably stupid and needy of me to think our friendship was in danger because I kissed him. But I couldn't handle losing him. I sit on his bed. "All right. I feel all the same things."

"Good. Now go get showered and let's get out of here."

"But I also felt something else. Something I wasn't expecting." His eyes are willing me to shut up now. "I liked it, Wylder. I didn't want you to stop touching me, and I didn't want to stop kissing you."

"You pulled back first," he reminds me. Then realizes what he's said. He closes his eyes, releases a lungful, and then joins me on the edge of the bed. "I liked it, too. It was weird, but good."

"You're weird, but good."

Normally, this is when he would push me off the bed or punch me in the arm, but I think he's afraid to touch me. Look at me even. "Are we going to be okay, Colt? I never thought I'd do something that could wreck our friendship, and I'm afraid if we keep going where that kiss leads, we will."

So he feels it, too. The possibility of more and the possibility of less. "We've been best friends for a long time, nothing is going to take that from us."

"Why are we talking about feelings right now? Wouldn't it be better if we just pretended it didn't happen and go fix shit and spit tobacco?"

"Neither of us chew tobacco, Wylder."

We sit in silence for a few minutes. Agonizing silence. "How's the foal doing?"

"Gonna be just fine."

"Good. You made the right decision that night. Giving her the chance to heal."

More quiet.

"Last night was the best sex of my life," I say. "I didn't know sex could be that good."

He nods, but since I'm not looking at him, I see it from the corner of my eye.

I hate small talk, but the big stuff is too important to talk about right now. And somehow leaving the conversation right now doesn't seem right either. I'm afraid of what will happen if I go and what will happen if I stay. Maybe talking about Bliss will help. "So, we're in a committed threesome now. Bliss, well, she's everything, right?"

He nods again. "What we had last night," he says finally, "that was more than good sex. We need to find a way to make her want to stay with us."

Well, now. That's a change in tune. "If she stays, we're a couple then...or whatever it's called for three. People are gonna talk."

"They already saw us dancing with her at the Hound. They're probably already talking."

In this town, yeah. "Do you care?"

"Nope. Do you?"

I shake my head. "So, people will probably assume you and I do stuff to each other too."

"Probably."

How have I never noticed before that he smells good? We use the same soap and shampoo, but somehow he smells different.

Get back to the subject at hand, Colt. "Do you care? What they assume?"

"Nope. Do you?"

"I did for a minute. This morning, when you were calling her bluff about touching me, I was thinking maybe I cared. Then you touched me for real, and I stopped caring what anyone outside of that bedroom might think. All I cared about was you and Bliss."

I never thought I'd enjoy a man's touch before. I never thought I'd be in the same room with Wylder while I was having sex, much less in the same girl. I never thought I'd feel his cum dripping onto my balls while we were inside that girl at the same time. I never thought I'd be looking into his eyes while we were in her. Or that I would kiss him.

"Wylder..."

"Can we just let it rest for a bit? I'm not disgusted and you're not disgusted. We have some kind of attraction, but we don't need to jump into anything too suddenlike. Wade into the water slowly is what I'm thinking."

"Fair enough. In the meantime, we can work on making sure Bliss never wants to leave the ranch."

He nods. "Now go fucking get dressed."

Chapter Twelve

Bliss

One month later

We're snuggled on the couch after dinner and chores and we're all acting normal. I mean, if you count me snuggling two big cowboys on the couch normal. But I feel like this is what a lot of people are looking for. We've been sleeping together for a month now. I know this because they brought me flowers and wished me a happy anniversary yesterday.

They dote on me, absolutely. They make me feel safe and cared for. And they are so darn easy on the eyes.

During a commercial, Colt picks up my feet and starts rubbing them. "Johnstone called me again today." I assume he's talking to Wylder since I don't know Johnstone. "He said he has a break in his schedule in September if we change our mind about building the sleeping quarters this year?"

Wylder lets out a beleaguered breath. "I just don't know."

"What is this about?" I ask. September is not that far away. Less than a month now.

Colt does something magical to the ball of my foot, and my whole body relaxes. "The next phase of the ranch needs more ranch hands. It's standard to include room and board. Have a bunkhouse on-site."

I look at Wylder. "Why don't you want to?"

He shrugs. I look at Colt. "Why doesn't he want to?"

"I don't speak for Wylder, darlin'." His voice is calm, but resolute. They've been backing each other up for a long time.

They make eye contact with each other, and I can tell that Wylder appreciates Colt's loyalty, too. But it stings a little. A lot. It's not my business, literally. I don't know anything about running a ranch other than feeding two cowboys. I'm not their girlfriend, not really. I know they aren't going to date anyone else while I'm here, I do trust that. But I'm still temporary. Why would either of them include me in their business decisions?

"I hate talking about this kind of stuff," Wylder says. The muscles in his jaw bunch up like he's holding himself in check. Like maybe that sentence leaked out when he didn't mean it to.

My stomach is churning, and it's silly. "It's okay. You don't have to."

The strain shows on Wylder's face. He's holding himself so tightly, like he's about to explode off the couch. "It's stupid," he says through a clenched jaw.

"It's not stupid," Colt says. "If it's not the right time—"

Wylder cuts him off. "I don't want to be responsible for anyone else, that's all."

This is about the night of the fire. Does he feel responsible for all that? He walks around balancing the world on his shoulders, so I'm sure he does take responsibility for things that even he couldn't have stopped. If there was a fire here, and someone in his employ got hurt or died, he'd totally feel responsible. The same way he feels he let his family down.

I bet Colt wanted to hire more guys in the beginning, but he's been patiently waiting for Wylder to be ready. Because that is how they work, whether they know it or not. Colt has immense compassion, and I think all he's wanted all these years is to take care of Wylder. Wylder is a natural leader, but he uses his impressive ego to protect himself from pain. And he feels an awful lot of pain. So, he's spent the last few years in his bubble of control and anything outside of that scares him—not that he could show it. Or even deal with it.

"That's fine," Colt says. "Besides, then we'd need to hire a full-time cook, too."

He leaves it hanging in the air like he's already moved on, but I'm shell-shocked. I put my hand over my heart to keep it in my ribcage, but then lower it quickly, hoping no one noticed. "What do you mean?"

Colt's gaze is inscrutable. "We'd need to feed the ranchers three squares a day."

Don't wish. Don't wish.

It's impossible not to wish. "I was wondering why you had such a great kitchen. It's part of the next phase, then? So, you're planning on having a cook live here also?"

"I guess so," Colt answers. "Eventually."

I pull my feet out of his lap. I need to rein in my brain, and I can't think when he's touching me. "And this person...they will plan all the menus and do all the shopping?"

He nods. "Sure. It'd be like what you do now, only for more people. Probably four ranchers to start, but the bunkhouse could house more later down the road. Of course, the cook won't have time for housework."

So what I do now minus the stuff I screw up. Full-time.

I can't imagine anything I'd enjoy more for a job. When I first thought about college, I thought that I would go on to culinary school. The career path didn't seem that stable, though. I didn't want something with a lot of highs and lows. Restaurants are fraught with drama, but what I yearned for was a life of pleasant...boredom. At least I did when I was finally out of the trailer park and someplace safe. Security meant not depending on anyone for anything I had. At the time, I thought all I wanted was a small apartment to go home to at five o'clock every evening. Maybe a cat. Netflix on weekends.

I never imagined dating. Or being creative like I get to be when I cook. I didn't think about kids or weddings. Just a job I could be good at and a safe place to sleep.

Don't wish. Don't wish.

Wylder is awfully quiet. I'm sitting right next to him, but I feel very far away.

For a minute, I imagine that things are different. That I've been here for years and this is my life now. That I've spent all day in the kitchen, and everyone loved my stew and French bread so much there were no leftovers. The other cowboys are all tucked into their bunkhouse, and mine are getting ready to take me upstairs and make love to me all night like we do every night. Maybe we even have a cat.

A dangerous longing fills my heart. *Don't wish, girl.* But I can't stop myself. It would be such a dream come true—a job I was good at and a safe place to sleep at night—but it would be more. There would be love. And belonging. There would be laughter. And hot sex all the time.

My brow furrows. I'm getting too far over my head in this. I promised myself I would enjoy every minute of this affair and not taint it with depressing thoughts about "after," but I need to do an intervention on myself for a bit. "You guys, I'm super tired. I think I'm just going to go crash for the night."

I start to sit up, but Wylder snags my hand, halting my progress. "Stay."

"I know you like it when I listen to your every command, but I'm too tired."

He draws a deep breath. "Stay. Don't go back to school."

Wylder

MY HEART TAKES A HARD hit when I look at the doubt in her eyes. I only ever want to see trust and happiness shining there.

"What?" she asks.

"The job is yours."

Colt turns off the television and sits up straight.

"The job?" Confusion is etched across her face. "The cook job? I won't be here."

I can't think of that. The idea of her not being here causes a physical ache in my chest. "We'll build the bunkhouse, hire the hands, and you can cook."

"Wylder, maybe she doesn't want to—"

"She wants to. Think about it, Bliss. You love that kitchen and you're an amazing cook, Stay."

She bites her lower lip. "What about school?"

Shit. I don't know why I acted so impulsively. Of course she's not going to quit school to be a cook. "Finish your classes."

"My accounting classes?"

"You don't want to be an accountant. But you should finish your degree. The job will be waiting for you."

She takes a shuddering breath. "And you? Will you both be waiting for me?"

"Is that what you want?" Colt asks, the hope in his voice reminds me of that evening with the wounded foal. How does he hold on to hope despite everything that's happened to him? How does he let down his guard so easily? Anyone could take his heart and hurt it, he just leaves it out. Bliss could break it. Hell, I could break it.

She's twisting the ends of her hair. "I don't know what I want."

"Yes, you do," I say bluntly. "You know exactly what you want, you're just too afraid to take it."

Her jaw works a bit, like she's trying to form words or maybe hold a few choice ones back. "Why do I always have to be the one that is vulnerable first?"

"What are you talking about? I just asked you to stay."

She shakes her head. "You offered me a job."

Colt is leaning in real close, his hand on her knee. "Do you want more than the job?"

"See? And then I have to tell you what I want *before* you offer it. Tell me what you want. Tell me how you feel. I understand that I was a virgin when we started and that I relied on you both for guidance and that I was naturally the one with the most fear. But now I think we're all evenly matched. None of us know how to put ourselves out there, and we're all scared. But what you are asking me to do is take all the risk of putting my feelings out first so you both can keep yours to yourself until it's safe. I'm afraid of what comes next, too. I'm afraid I'll tell you how I feel and be rejected or maybe hurt someone." Her hand shakes as she brings it to her face to wipe a tear threatening to fall. "I don't know why I'm even having this discussion. You two have been best friends for twenty years and haven't even been honest with each other about how you feel or what you want. Why would you open up to me?"

Colt's hand squeezes her leg gently. "What are you talking about?"

"It's been a month and the only contact you've had in the bedroom is eye sex. I know you are both interested in going further with each other, but nobody will say it first. You just look at each other intensely and wait for the other to show his cards."

I can't sit still any longer. This situation is out of control again. "Fine. I want you to stay because I can't imagine a day without you in it. Does that satisfy your need for a sacrifice?"

"Fifty percent," she answers, and then turns to Colt and waits.

"Hell, darlin'. If I told you how I really feel, you'd run screaming into the night."

"Tell. Me." Her voice is quiet, but firm.

He takes her pretty face in his hands. "Bliss Camden, I fell head over hoof for you the day I gave you the tour of the kitchen. Yes, I want you to stay. Yes, I'll wait for you as long as you need to finish what's out there in the world before you're ready for what's right here. And yes, what I want is forever. I want to put babies in you and grow old with you at our side."

Her eyes widen. Mine do, too.

"Oh," she says simply.

"Yeah, oh," he repeats and kisses her. "Told you it was scary. Want to hear something else?"

"There's more?"

He turns to me. "I want to explore what we started last month."

"Colt...I..."

"I want you, Wylder."

Colt

THIS IS IT, I GUESS. I said my piece. I feel like a weight has been lifted off my shoulders. I spent that first day trying to figure if I was magically gay overnight, and it finally occurred to me that I was just me, and no other labels were important. My heart has always belonged to Wylder.

I just didn't know it was his. Until Bliss came along, there was no one who ever got close to my heart. Now I know why. I didn't *want* anyone to come between the two of us. It wasn't until she came into our lives that the clouds parted. She's the key to everything.

I've done everything in my power to stay in his life since we were kids. To be a part of his every day. I love him as deeply as a man can love, and I'd like to find new ways to express it.

But it's scary as fuck putting it out there.

"You want me?" His eyes are shining fiercely, but he's not telling me yes or no.

"I do," I say simply. "She's right. I've been waiting for a green light or something from you since we talked about that kiss. But now I'm saying it for the record. I want you."

He turns to Bliss. "And that's okay with you?"

"Again, Wylder, you're asking me to tell you how I feel so you know how much of yourself you can reveal."

"Fuck." He paces some more. "I hate talking about feelings. How am I supposed to know how I feel?"

She stands up and puts her arms around him. He stops pacing, but he's stiff and uncomfortable. "Okay, okay. I'll take a turn. I don't want to go back to school in September. I feel like I should finish my degree, but maybe I can do it online or something. I want to stay here, with both of you, because this is where I belong. Where I feel safe. The thought of anyone else working in my kitchen makes me want to throw the cast iron pan into a wall. And the idea of anyone else in your bed makes me feel like murdering someone." My heart lifts at her words. She wants to stay. She wants us. "And I loved watching you two together. I don't want to just be the object of both of your affections—I want to be a circle where we all take care of each other."

Wow. Her vision of what the future could be is even more awesome than the one I was devising.

Wylder lets out a deep breath, relaxing a bit in her arms but looking at me. "Fine. Yeah, I can't get my mind off what happened between us. And yeah, I'm curious. Hell, you know how I feel about you, Colt."

I nod, letting him off the hook. A little. "I do."

"I don't actually know...how it would work. In bed with both of you that way. I don't know how...how it would work. But I want to try."

"We don't need to rush anything," I tell him.

I join their hug, still holding myself a little apart from Wylder. "Is anyone else feeling horny as hell right now?"

"If I say yes, can we stop talking about feelings?" Wylder asks.

We agree to take it to the bedroom. When we get to Bliss's room, we stand next to her bed facing each other and strip ourselves slowly. It feels more like more than just getting naked. It feels like getting...defenseless.

Also horny.

But I feel like I'm shedding off more than the protection of clothes. When we're finally naked, I let myself look at Wylder's body.

I pull him out of my mouth but keep a firm grip on his shaft. Too firm, but he's not complaining. My tongue swirls around his heavy sac, tasting him, knowing him so intimately now.

I tried to tell myself when we first started this threesome with Bliss that it was just sex, and sex feels good and it doesn't matter if there are accidental touches or things get too close. All that mattered was pleasure and our girl. But it matters a lot. It matters to me that this is Wylder in my hands, under my tongue. It's his scent wrapping around my senses. It doesn't take anything away from what I feel for Bliss. If anything, it makes me feel stronger about the both of them.

This wouldn't be happening with anyone else. It has to be Bliss and Wylder. It will always be Bliss and Wylder. She needs to be part of this. "Darlin', you're too far away over there."

"I want to watch."

"You can watch. I just want you close by." I need them both right now.

She settles next to me on the floor, and I lick back up my best friend's rod, moving up to the swollen, dark head. I slide him back into my mouth. His moans get louder, raspier. I'm ravenous now, sucking on him with total abandon.

"You're going to make me come. Is that what you want?"

I moan around him again. I need it.

Bliss rubs my back. "Yes, Wylder. We want you to come."

"I'm going to give you what you want, Colt. I'm going to fill your throat. Fuck!" He roars as his orgasm erupts in my mouth, filling me. Over and over he squirts, each shudder adding more. Jesus, how do people do this? There's so much cum. I'm trying to swallow it down without choking. I remember Bliss taking all of me down that first night and I'm in even more awe of her now.

I've tasted him before, not this much at once, but in the weeks we've been part of a triad, there have been traces of him left behind when I kiss Bliss or get her pussy ready with my tongue for another round.

But drinking him in is so satisfying, it's only now that I am reminded of my own need to come.

I'm hot and aching to feel him inside me. But I'm not ready for that just yet.

"That was amazing," Bliss says. She kisses me deeply, taking into her the taste of our lover's cum. God. I need to come. Now. I pull her onto my lap and thrust into her tight, wet sheath. She comes fast when I add pressure to her clit, her inner muscles squeezing me as she rides out some good, hard bounces.

I flip her over and grab her hips, pulling her straight back onto me, wrapping her pretty, dark hair around my fist and pulling her head back. "Tell me you're staying with us," I demand, fucking her almost violently.

"I'm staying. I'm never leaving. Oh, God."

Wylder shakes off his come-coma and slides to his knees in front of her, lifting her chin so she'll look at him. "Oh, he's fucking you hard, kitten. Do you like that? Your poor little pussy."

"Oh, God." She's trying really hard to keep looking at him, but I'm hammering her hard and her body is getting jerked back and forth. "I love it. I love what you both do to me so much."

I'm holding out as long as I can. Wylder and I make eye contact and my spine starts tingling.

"Fuck her, Colt. Fuck our woman. Make her come again all over your cock."

I grunt, trying to get even deeper.

"Stretch out that sweet pussy. Jesus, she's taking that big, thick dick, isn't she? Are you going to come again, angel?"

I pull her hair and he holds her throat the way she likes. She likes feeling owned by us. That's when she feels the freest to be completely uninhibited. She stirs every dark desire I ever had. Makes me feel so rough. I grip her hip in my hand so firmly I know I'll be leaving my mark on her. Her inner muscles clench, squeezing me until I can't hold back any longer. As she comes, I pour all of myself into her. She's changed everything, the catalyst to the fire that consumes us all now. I wrap my arms around her chest and press her tightly against me with a satisfied groan, my own breath sawing sharp edges into my lungs. "Did I hurt you?"

"No, well, yes, but the good kind. I'm good. I promise."

"You're better than good, darlin'."

We sit up and Wylder wraps a blanket around her shoulders. He meets my eyes and the floor drops out from under me. He's looking at me with something new. It's almost fragile, vulnerable. For a man who'd do just about anything not to be vulnerable to anyone or anything, it means something. Something I guess I've been working toward since the day we met. I know already that he trusts me, that he'd do anything for me, but there's always been a piece of him that he held back.

I may have given him a blow job, but with that one look, he just gave me everything.

Chapter Thirteen

Bliss

Three months later

I'm surprised to find my men at the kitchen table when I come in from the farmer's market. "Oh, good, I could use some brawny manpower to help with the big box of squash I got at...the..." my words trail off when I realize they are not alone. I set the bag down carefully, willing my knees to stop shaking. My heart wobbles against my ribs. I think I might throw up. "Mom, what are you doing here?"

Her voice rasps out, "Is that any way to say hello to your mother?" To Wylder she says, "Well, I guess we were always more like sisters anyway."

Colt stands up and comes to the doorway I'm still stuck in, providing support immediately just by standing at my side. I must look like I'm going to fall over. I certainly feel like it. I guess I just never anticipated my past meeting my present like this. I think I hoped it would never happen at all.

My mother looks like a light breeze could blow her away. She's skeletal thin, her blonde hair frizzy on the edges, but two inches of dark roots means she hasn't even been able to afford drugstore hair dye for a few months. Or she's given up caring.

She's wearing long sleeves, but the way she keeps scratching at her arms is a clue to how messed up she is.

How did she even find me? I've only communicated with her by text for the last year. And that's only if she doesn't run out of minutes. Which she hasn't this summer because I filled her phone card several times.

"This is a sweet set-up you have here, baby girl. I hope these nice young men have been taking care of you."

That's what she thinks men are for. To take care of her. She told me when I was sixteen years old that pussy was currency for survival. She paid for things she needed in trade, things like the rent. That same night, she told me sucking cock was for life's little luxuries. That's how she afforded cigarettes and vodka. She was convinced she was being a good mother by telling me how life really is. That I should get what I could while I was still young and my currency was worth the most.

By the time I got out of the trailer, she was trading her body for drugs mostly.

"I'm so proud of you, baby girl." Her words are like a slap. All my life, I waited for those words. Pride in me, even an interest in my life. But now the words are unwelcome.

"You should be proud," Wylder says. He's sizing her up, taking her measure. He's holding his body loose, like he's totally relaxed, but I can tell he's coiled up tight inside and ready to spring if need be.

"Mom, why are you here?"

"Well, baby girl, you had so many nice things to say about this place. How much you loved the fresh air. You're right, it sure is beautiful here." She's not looking out the window, and she's not looking at me. She's looking at Colt standing next to me. "You sure have done well for yourself. Surprised me, even. I figured you'd waste away your youth in a dark office with only your computer to keep you company. And here you are, in a mansion with two handsome cowboys all to yourself."

"Mom..."

"Such a good girl. You always were, though. A little goody two-shoes. But now look at you."

I feel the blood leaving my face. She thinks I'm trading my pussy like currency. She thinks I'm just like her. Am I?

"Ms. Camden, you seem like a real nice lady," Wylder starts in his cold, commanding voice, "so I'm sure you just haven't noticed that you are distressing your daughter."

She's cowed by his voice. Who isn't? Well, I'm not. Not really. Well, okay, sometimes. But only in bed.

"Guys, I still have groceries in the Jeep. If you wouldn't mind…"

Colt's body tightens next to me. "I think one of us should stay in here with you and your guest."

"I'm fine."

"Of course she's fine. I'm her mother. She couldn't be safer with anyone than she is with me."

I see Wylder struggle to not pick her up and throw her out the window. I'm not doing a very good job of hiding my uneasiness at being with my mom. They are not her biggest fans, either.

Reluctantly, they go out to the Jeep leaving me alone with the woman who raised me to be afraid of my own sexuality. "Why are you really here?"

"Which one are you fucking?"

I close my eyes. "Do you need money? What?"

"I know you're not fucking them both. Hell, I'm surprised you nabbed one. You must have finally taken my lessons to heart. My guess is Mr. Colt. The other one would eat you up and spit you out." She coughs too long and too harshly. All those luxuries she got on her knees for must be catching up to her lungs. "He won't marry you," she says finally. "Not that you don't have fine birthing hips and all, but a man like that isn't going to marry the fat cook, so I hope you're doing better than I did at saving for a rainy day. Of course, you don't have the handicap of having to raise a kid at the same time."

My blood turns to ice. "Handicap?"

"No offense."

I have to fight the urge to run to my room and hide. But I'm not a kid anymore. This is my home, not hers. "I took none of your lessons to heart, Mom. I'm nothing like you."

She moves fast. One minute she's in the chair, next she's standing in front of me poking my chest. "You're just like me. I know you always thought you were better than me, but you're just as much a whore as I ever was. Maybe now you'll have some respect. You think I enjoyed fucking Greasy Greg when I didn't have enough money for rent? You think I liked blowing all the fat, married men whose wives wouldn't do it? I hated every minute on my knees. But that's what we got to work with in this life."

"You're sick. I mean that literally, Mom. There is something wrong in your head and you tried your best to make it wrong in mine, too, didn't you? Would it make you feel better if I turned into the town tramp instead of a college graduate? Would you like it better if I had an unplanned pregnancy like you did? Well, sorry, I'm not going to turn out like you. And when I have kids, I'll make sure they have security and love."

Her nostrils flare. "He won't marry you. He'll get tired of fucking you eventually, and then you'll lose this cushy job. The one you quit school over, so don't get so high and mighty with me, Ms. "College Graduate." And then you'll either live in a trailer in town, I saw some behind the tavern. Or you'll move back in with me thinking I'll help you raise your little brat. That's the life we get. That's where our genetics take us. So you might want to think twice about talking shit about me now in case you need me later."

The idea of her near any child of mine brings maternal instincts I didn't know I had right to the front. "You will never even see any children I have. I don't know why I've been sending you money while I've been at school and here. I don't know why I ever thought I needed to keep in contact with you or make sure you were all right. I thought I had some obligation, I guess. But the last few months have really taught me that everything about you is unhealthy. You don't know how to love. Not yourself and certainly not your own child." I take a deep breath like I've been drowning for years and just got to the surface. "But I do know how to love. And I know that I have to love myself in order to really love someone else. I know that now because two men, yes both of them, mother, showed me what I was worth. Every day, they show me."

"How am I the tramp if you're the one fucking two men?"

"You have warped ideas about sex and you did your best to warp mine. But giving yourself to someone is different from trading your body for something."

The skin across her face is stretched so tight I worry that her cheekbones are going to poke through. "You ungrateful little bitch."

The slap across my face shocks me more than hurts me. She doesn't have much strength. Not like she used to. Not like the good old days.

If anything, she just slapped some sense into me.

"I'm going to marry them both, Mama. And we're all three going to live in this big happy house filled with as many babies as they'll give me. I'm going to enter my blueberry pie into the state fair and learn to ride a horse properly. I'll finish my degree because I'm smart and too close to walk away from it, but I won't be moldering away in a dark office. I'll use my accounting skills to help my husbands run this place. I'm going to be just fine, despite you. Because I love them both more than anything and they've taught me how to trust them and trust myself."

A masculine throat clearing brings my attention to the door where both my men are standing with their hearts in their eyes. Colt addresses my mother, "Ms. Camden, a taxi will meet you out front to take you back to town. The bus leaves town in the morning, but we paid for a room for you across from the station for the night. You're not to come back to the ranch."

"You're dead to me. I shoulda left you in a dumpster when I had you." She bristles when Wylder grabs her arm gently to steer her out of the kitchen but goes. He's kind of hard to argue with.

As soon as she's gone, my legs give out. Colt is right there, scooping me up and carrying me to the bathroom. While he's running the bath, Wylder comes in. His eyes are soft when he kneels in front of me. "I'm so proud of you, kitten. That was amazing."

"You guys are amazing. I would never have been able to do that if it weren't for you. I love you both so much. I don't know what's kept me from saying I love you all this time, I knew it from the beginning, I think. I'm sorry you had to hear it that way instead of me just saying the words."

Colt kneels next to Wylder. They both have a hand on each of my knees. "I love you, darlin'. I always will. And Wylder, I'm in love with you, too. I don't know if I'd say it was from the beginning. I've always loved you, but now, it's more. It has been for a while."

Wylder looks at Colt's hand on my knee, but not at either of our faces. "Hell, the two of you are like thorns in my side." He puts his hand over Colt's. "After the night when...when everything was taken from me, I slipped into a dark place. A place where the only voice I heard was Colt trying to bring me back." He finally raises his eyes to Colt's face. "You saved my life. You dragged my ass back into the light even though I didn't want it. I knew what I felt after that was more than friendship, but I didn't know what to call it. How to feel about it. And I didn't want to feel too much anyway. I thought I'd be better off just working hard and making my folks proud when they looked down on me." He looks at me then. "And then we got a sassy little housekeeper." I smile. "Bliss, you made us brave enough to open our hearts. I love you and I love Colt. And that damn bathtub is about to spill over the edge."

Colt hurries to turn the water off. "Do you mean it, Wylder? I know we've both been okay with fooling around, but do you really love me?"

Wylder stands, bringing me up with him. "Of course I do. Now about this getting married and filling the house with babies..."

I cover my face. "You heard the whole thing?"

"I heard every detail of my dream life repeated to me in your voice," Colt says. "I'd be the happiest man alive if we all got married and filled this house with babies and blueberry pie."

Wylder puts his sturdy arms around both of our waists, pulling us in to him. "I am especially excited about the part where I don't have to do the accounting bullshit anymore. Say the word, Bliss and you can do whatever you want with the books."

My heart is so full. "Are we really going to do this?"

"I'd say we are already doing it." Wylder brushes a kiss to my temple. "I'm sorry we even let your mom into the house."

"I'm not. I needed to have some closure on that part of my life."

Colt starts fiddling with the button on my pants. "Why don't you take a bath before the water gets too cold? We'll put the groceries away and then we'll have a big ol' lovefest."

They get me in the tub, and they leave, holding hands. That's a new thing. They don't have a problem touching each other with hands and mouths in bed, but they don't show affection outside of it, usually.

Epilogue

Wylder

"You're sure?" My hand is stopped halfway to the cupboard.

"I've seen you looking at my ass. Yes, I'm sure. I want to try it. If Bliss can take it, I can."

I want to, damn, I sure as hell want to. We've done a lot of stuff, my favorite is always when one of us is in her pussy and one of us is in her ass. I love feeling his cock sliding against mine. I love the three of us being so close. But neither of us have crossed the bridge to each other's ass yet. There's no rush, it's not like our sex life is getting stale or anything.

"We've watched the movies. They seem to like it," he assures me.

Like because we've watched gay porn a few times, we're experts now. "They're actors."

"They're not very good actors. You can tell which ones like it a lot and which ones think they look like they do. Besides, the one doing the fucking always looks happy to be there. And that will be you. At least for now."

I close the cupboard, forgetting what I opened it for. "I don't want to hurt you, Colt."

"Wylder, don't make me beg." He grins, knowing that comment just made me hard as a rock.

My heart races, the thrill of the forbidden coursing through me. I want to fuck him. I have for a while. I want to be balls-deep while his tight channel clenches around my cock. I want to mark him as mine the same way I always want to mark Bliss. "Maybe I will make you beg.

Would you like that, cowboy?" I use my body to pin him against the fridge, not trying to hide the bulge in my pants that he put there.

The glint in his eyes mirrors my own fierce need. He grumbles something I can't quite hear, and then pulls me into a rough kiss.

When we both pull back, I know it's going to be tonight. I'm scared as hell that my life is too perfect. I couldn't survive it if I lost either of them. But I'm through with being a coward. "Tonight, I'm finally gonna know what it feels like to be inside you."

We somehow finish putting the groceries away and go find our woman. She's tying her robe, so I grab her wrists and Colt undoes all her hard work, spreading the panels open and revealing all her milky white flesh. I keep a tight hold of her as he yanks the garment over her shoulders.

"Spread your legs and show Colt your pretty pink pussy." She opens her legs. "Wider. That's a good girl." I transfer her wrists to one hand and use the other to cup one of her gorgeous tits. "Taste her," I tell him.

He's on his knees with his face buried in her right away. When he lifts one of her legs over his shoulder for better access, she has to lean further back into me or she'd fall down. He devours her like an animal until she's panting.

"Look at his face, Bliss. Do you see how wet you're making his face? Such a naughty wet girl."

He growls into her and she starts coming like fireworks. When she's a boneless heap of woman, I pick her up and carry her to the bed. I cup her jaw. "I love you. I love watching you come."

She smiles. "I feel like a princess. A filthy, naughty princess, but a princess."

I stand up all the way and Colt kisses me, sharing the taste of her honeyed juices with me. I'm so fucking hard. Bliss is working both our zippers, so we separate so we can take down our jeans. Once we're naked, she reaches for both our cocks. "I love the way you both feel. But even more, I love the way you taste."

We stand as close together as we can so she can get that taste of cocks she wants so bad. I don't know how much longer I can stand it. Bliss is alternating between us, long, slow sucks deep in her hot, wet mouth, then cold air when she wraps her full lips around Colt.

Colt and I catch gazes. He's got that look that I just want to keep on him all the time. Dirty, raw, and so in his element. Our mouths find each other, the turning of our upper bodies making it easier for Bliss to wrap both her hands around our cocks like they are one. She can't possibly get them both in her mouth, but bless that girl, she tries.

The kiss quickly deepens, pulling and tugging at the line between my heart and my dick. My whole world is in this room.

"Baby, you're gonna make me come too soon," I tell Bliss.

"Why is that a problem?" She slurps a little more.

"Because I promised Colt something special tonight."

She stops slurping. "Tonight?"

"Tonight."

We get on the bed with her. Colt eases onto his back. "Come here, darlin'." He pulls her up until she's straddling his head facing me, and then he starts eating her out. Her eyes roll back and I'm mesmerized. I want to keep watching, but I promised him, didn't I? And I'm a man who keeps his promises.

I straddle his center, our dicks lined up against each other.

"Ungh," he moans into Bliss's pussy.

Yeah, it does feel good. Electric. I take us both in two hands and start stroking. It's so intense, and jolts of pleasure zap through me. Bliss is riding his face, losing her inhibitions, and mine are getting swept out to sea also.

I move against him with a grinding motion, driving my cock into his abs with almost brute force, my precum smearing on his stomach. Jesus, I'm going to blow, and we've barely started.

Without fully lifting my body, I reposition so my dick is now pressing against his again, and it takes everything in me to keep from exploding right now. His balls are rubbing against the root on the underside of my cock. He feels so fucking good.

He can't see anything, but he's not complaining. Bliss is grinding on his face, and his hands reach up to squeeze her perfect breasts. "You're perfect," I tell her.

She comes. One of her small ones. Like an appetizer. Or maybe more like dessert after she came hard a few minutes ago. I can hear Colt's deep, rough breaths.

"When I fuck you, Colt, I'm going to fill you with my cum. I'm going to fuck you so hard, you'll feel me for days." I reach for the lube and get ready, nervous like the first time I had sex. "Do you want my big cock right now? Are you ready?"

His face is shiny from Bliss, and I hear the affirmative in his moan. Bliss pauses her humping and watches me as I push his knees up, opening him to me, and work slowly into his tight ass. He's been using some toys the last few weeks to stretch himself a little, but he's still really fucking tight. Bliss climbs off him, which is good. I want to see his face. Make sure I'm not hurting him.

I groan, my cock pulsing inside him. When I'm sheathed deep inside to my balls, I shudder.

"So good," he breathes.

Thank fuck.

He brings his legs around my waist and holds me tightly to him. I begin to move in and out, in slow, deep thrusts. She's got a hand on him now, using gentle strokes and his precum as lube for the handjob. My hands lock together with his, and he tightens his grip as I move faster, harder. Over and over I slam into him, the sounds of flesh slapping against flesh fills the room as both of us meet each other with unbridled need.

The fire in his eyes riles me up even more. I take Bliss's lips hungrily, swallowing her moan as I thrust deep inside Colt. I break the kiss.

"Sweet girl, you better start jacking his cock hard. Things are about to get interesting."

He can't control the sounds he's making anymore as my fat cock grazes him just right and her hand jacks him roughly. They are guttural and primal sounds. I respond with grunts of my own. Bliss is pumping her hand in short, hard strokes, bringing him to orgasm all over her hand and his stomach. I bring her hand to my mouth and lick him off her fingers.

Colt and I are slick with sweat, coating each other as we slide with each thrust. "You want my cum, cowboy?"

"Give it to me."

I lean down to his ear, slowing my strokes, deep, slow, and long. "Beg."

"Give me your cum, Wylder. Give it to me."

I increase my pace and bite his neck, losing myself in his body. With a growl, I lodge my cock deep inside him, harder than I've ever done with a woman. My body shudders violently, quaking uncontrollably as my cock jerks over and over.

When we can breathe, I ease out slowly and we pin our woman to the bed, sharing her pussy with our tongues until she's screaming gibberish. When she falls asleep, I watch Colt watch her. He's so lost in love it makes my fool heart grow even more.

When I think about how the two of them grew up, I question again how either of them are able to look at the future with anything but distrust. Colt's parents abandoned him completely, and I have to wonder if Bliss would have been better off if her mother had done the same. Yet here they are, trusting each other, trusting me, trusting a future with babies and pie and love.

I had a great childhood. My parents had plenty of love to go around, giving a lot to Colt whenever he was over. They taught me how to be a man. Would they be proud right now? Of the ranch, yes. Would they understand my relationships with Colt and Bliss? Or would they have turned away from me? I want to believe they would have supported me. I know they would love Bliss and they already thought of Colt like a son.

A soft snore tells me Colt has followed Bliss into slumber. My demons are quiet, and I'm sated for now; I should take a nap myself. I have everything a man could want, though, and that makes it hard to rest. There are plans to make. A wedding to plan. Rings to buy. We'll need to make sure Bliss is an equal partner in the business so she'll be taken care of if anything happens to us. I know we can't all be legal spouses, so we'll need to find the best way to take care of each other that way.

Babies. Hell, I never thought I'd want those. Not after I lost my pregnant sister. But all at once it hits me what's different, what's new. Hope. For the first time since everything in me went black, I've found that hope I used to marvel at Colt for having. He showed Bliss and me how to find it, somehow.

I think he kept my broken pieces for me all these years, kept them safely locked in his own heart until Bliss gave us the key to unlock it all.

And now, I have a hankering for pie.

SIGH I hope you enjoyed watching Bliss and her two cowboys fall in love as much as I enjoyed discovering their story and writing it down. Filthy sweet, right? If you enjoyed *All at Once*, please consider leaving a review so other readers who love steamy romance with an a sticky sweet romance can find their new obsession.

The swooning doesn't have to end here for you, though. I'm a fan of awkward, nerdy heroines and burly, dominating alpha heroes who have the ooey-gooiest hearts ever. We like to call them: alphamallows.

ALL AT ONCE

IF YOU'RE TIRED OF billionaires, maybe you're ready for some real men. Dirty, hardworking, and good with their hands are the kind of heroes you'll find in the *Blue Collar Bad Boy Series*. These guys aren't cultured. They are hot *AF* alpha heroes who know how to take care of the slightly nerdy women they fall for. For reals, this series is more fun than you knew you were missing. And they don't need to be read in order.

So which blue collar bad boy will you choose next? They are all rough, raw, and surprisingly sweet.

Like...the roadhouse bouncer and the actuarial sciences student in *Bounced*[1].

Or...the carpenter and the Jeopardy! nerd in *Nailed*[2].

Perhaps...the oil rigger and the kindergarten teacher in *Drilled*[3].

Mayhap...the tow truck driver and the sorority uptown girl in *Wrecked*[4].

Surely...the brick layer hot single dad and the babysitter in *Laid*[5].

How about...a returning military hero and the wallflower at Christmas in *Tagged*[6]?

Or...the farmer who needs a wife and wants the curvy waitress in *Plowed*[7]?

Or...the hot rancher trying to convince the city girl to stay in *Bucked*[8]?

Maybe...the bomb squad cop and his pregnant neighbor? Did I mention she's a virgin? You read that right. Try *Banged*[9].

---

1. https://books2read.com/Bounced
2. https://books2read.com/Nailed
3. https://books2read.com/Drilled
4. https://books2read.com/wrecked
5. https://books2read.com/laid
6. https://books2read.com/tagged
7. https://books2read.com/plowed
8. https://books2read.com/bucked

And surely...the modern day Viking bartender and the bookworm virgin in *Tapped*[10]?

---

9. https://books2read.com/banged
10. https://books2read.com/Tapped-A-Blue-Collar-Bad-Boy-Book

About the author

Like first times? Forbidden fruit? *Yes, please.*

Love a hot, dominant alpha claiming what's his? *Fuck, yeah.*

Want to watch him fall hard for the sweetest fantasy he didn't know he needed? Me too!

I'm Brill Harper and I love happily ever afters, smokin' hot bad boys, and quirky, often nerdy, heroines that I'd love to be friends with off page. These ladies are not perfect—but they're perfect for one man—and he's always sexy AF.

Seriously—these heroes only have one weakness, and it's sticky, sweet love. They don't let anything stand in the way of taking what belongs to them. When it comes to the women they love, it's hard cocks, dirty talk, and soft, mushy heart feels.

*Brill is a sooper sekrit penname for a better-known author who just can't handle all the dirty. She can't handle it...but can you?

Facebook [11]

Brill's Bites Newsletter[12] Readers get bonus content for free, as well as sneak peeks of upcoming books and exclusive giveaways!

BookBub[13]

---

11. https://www.facebook.com/Brill-Harper-1931520800417566/
12. https://mailchi.mp/f440d4dede17/rockstarreaders
13. https://www.bookbub.com/authors/brill-harper

Also by Brill Harper

Blue Collar Bad Boys
Bounced: A Blue Collar Bad Boys Book
Nailed: A Blue Collar Bad Boys Book
Drilled: A Blue Collar Bad Boys Book
Wrecked: A Blue Collar Bad Boys Book
Laid: A Blue Collar Bad Boys Book
Tagged
Plowed
Bucked: A Blue Collar Bad Boys Book
Banged: A Blue Collar Bad Boys Book
Tapped: A Blue Collar Bad Boy Book

It's Complicated
All Together
All at Once

Love in Brazen Bay
Wrong Number Text
The Right Stuff
So Wrong It's Right

Don't Get Me Wrong

Standalone
Dirty Jobs: a Blue Collar Bad Boys Collection
Notch on His Bedpost
Honeymoon With The Prince:: A Modern Day Fairy Tale
Good Girl

Watch for more at https://brillharper.com.